MURDER ON ICE

After her boyfriend runs out on her with the contents of their joint bank account, Kat Latcham has no choice but to return to the tiny village of Millford Magna where she grew up. The place, she complains, is not so much sleepy as comatose, and she longs for something exciting to happen. But when she and her childhood friend Will discover a body, and Will's father is suspected of murder, Kat suddenly realises she should have heeded the saying, 'Be careful what you wish for'.

PAULA WILLIAMS

MURDER ON ICE

Complete and Unabridged

LINFORD
Leicester

First published in Great Britain

First Linford Edition
published 2014

A catalogue record for this book is available
from the British Library.

ISBN 978–1–4448–1979–3

Published by
F. A. Thorpe (Publishing)
Anstey, Leicestershire

Set by Words & Graphics Ltd.
Anstey, Leicestershire
Printed and bound in Great Britain by
T. J. International Ltd., Padstow, Cornwall

This book is printed on acid-free paper

1

It's not quite true to say that nothing ever happens in the little Somerset village of Millford Magna. Back in 1685, the notorious Judge Jeffreys hanged a couple of men from the village from the large oak tree that used to stand by the pond for their part in the Monmouth Rebellion. Their sorry remains were left in the tree as a grim warning to anyone who might be tempted to take up arms against the King.

It must have worked because no one in the village has taken up arms against the King or anyone else since then. Although, in recent memory, the Vicar came pretty close when John Fleming's cows got into the Vicarage garden and trampled his prize begonias a week before the village Flower and Produce Show.

Apart from that, Millford Magna was as quiet — and some would say, dull — as the grave.

But all that was about to change. Because someone in Millford Magna had murder on their mind. Or, to be specific, one carefully planned, undetectable murder. They spent most of their waking moments thinking about it, planning it, imagining what life would be like before, during and after. Especially after.

It was a shining beacon of light in a life made dark by constant frustrations, humiliations and disappointments.

Murder was easy. Once you'd worked out how to do it. And, more to the point, how to get away with it.

2

Kat Latcham's hands shook with the effort of controlling her anger as she stared down at the thin, crepey neck, stretched out invitingly in front of her. It was tempting, oh so tempting. Just one quick movement. That was all it would take. Of course, she'd be careful to make it look like an accident. It was a risk, but, she reckoned, one worth taking.

'Come on, Katie. Stop daydreaming,' her mother called sharply, as if reading her mind. 'You haven't been away that long that you've forgotten how to shampoo, have you?'

'And you watch what you're doing with that water, young lady,' Elsie Flintlock said. 'I don't want that shooting down my neck. Not at my age. I could end up with them newmonials again and the doctor said they nearly did for me last winter.'

'I'm sorry? New what?'

'Elsie had a bad bout of pneumonia last

winter,' her mother said.

'New what,' Elsie cackled. 'You were miles away then, girlie. Keep up.'

Would that I was miles away, Kat wanted to say, but didn't dare. Not with her mother listening to her every word. Would that I was somewhere where people called me Kat, not Katie. Where they treated me like an adult, not like I was still a little kid. Where they 'got' the way I dressed and thought it was cool, not asked if I'd taken to wearing Grandad's cast-offs.

In short, Kat longed to be anywhere that was not here. In Chez Cheryl's, her mother's hairdressing salon. Millford Magna's top hairdressing establishment, according to the faded sign on the front gate. It was, in fact, Millford Magna's only hairdressing salon, and was established in Cheryl's front room, which caused a bit of a space problem when circumstances beyond her control forced Kat to give up her flat in Bristol and return to live with her parents while she recovered from a temporary financial crisis.

'Come on now, you still haven't answered my question,' Elsie persisted. 'Some folk are saying that fancy boyfriend of yours, the one with sandy eyelashes and the phoney posh accent, gave you the heave ho. Is that right? Mind you, I always say, never trust a man with sandy eyelashes.'

'Let me know if this is too hot, Mrs Flintlock.' If Kat's voice sounded strangled, it was because it was difficult to speak normally through rigidly clenched jaws. 'And no, he did not kick me out. I walked out.'

She could have said that she'd walked out because he went off with her best friend, who also happened to be her flat mate. Not only that, but the lowlife took her car with him. And that he left her more broke than broken-hearted. But she wouldn't, not in a million years. Not to Millford Magna's gossipmonger in chief. If spreading gossip was an Olympic sport, Elsie Flintlock would be a quadruple gold medallist. They had no need of super fast broadband in the village. Elsie spread gossip faster than the speed of light.

'I dare say Will Fleming will be pleased to hear that,' Elsie cackled. 'Poor lad. I reckon he — ow! That's really cold. What are you trying to do? I'll end up with double newmonials at this rate. Here, Cheryl, that daughter of yours is trying to kill me, she is. I'm freezing to death here.'

'It's all right, Elsie. I'll take over now.' Cheryl elbowed Kat out of the way and took over at the basin. She gave her a look that said 'you and I will be having words about this later, young lady' and hissed in a low voice that had Elsie's ears wiggling with the effort of straining to hear: 'You go and see to Marjorie Hampton. Just take the perm rollers out and rinse off. Do you think you can manage that without drowning the poor soul?'

'If you'll come with me, Mrs Hampton,' Kat said. 'I'll rinse you off. Mum will be with you soon.'

Marjorie Hampton was a big-boned, awkward woman with a long horsey face and long horsey teeth. She towered above Kat as she followed her across to the corner of the room where the basins were. 'It's Miss Hampton,' she said in a firm, no-nonsense voice. 'I was never foolish enough to marry.'

Kat heard Elsie Flintlock splutter as Marjorie Hampton took the seat at the next basin. 'They saw her coming and ran a mile, more like it,' she muttered as Cheryl wrapped her head in a towel and led her away before she could do any more mischief. But, thankfully, Marjorie didn't hear. Like Elsie, she talked non-stop. But at least, in her case, she wasn't interested in Kat's love life, or lack of it. In fact the only thing Marjorie wanted to talk about was Marjorie.

She was an incomer. A person has to live in Millford Magna for at least twenty years before they're considered part of the village and she'd moved into the Old Forge at the far end of the village less than two years ago. And a terrible mess the previous owners had left it in, apparently. As to what they'd done to the bathroom, that, according to Marjorie, didn't bear thinking about.

But incomer or not, in that short time, she'd woven herself into the very fabric of village life. President of the Women's

Institute and organiser of the church flower rota ('Well, someone has to do it and goodness knows, the vicar's wife is about as useful as a paper parasol in the thunderstorm'). Not only that, she was chair of the Floral Arts Society and something to do with the Ramblers Association. There was, it appeared, not a single pie in Millford Magna, that didn't have one of Marjorie Hampton's long, bony fingers in it.

Kat relaxed a little as she heard, rather than listened to, Marjorie's voice going on and on, while Kat unwound the rollers from her blue-rinsed hair. The shade was called Midnight Hyacinth, but the poor woman looked more like a fancy new strain of blue cauliflower than a hyacinth.

'And so I said to him, I'll see you there,' Marjorie went on. And on. 'And I'll want an explanation. It's about time someone around here found the courage to stand up to him. And stand up to him I will. He'll find once I've got my dander up, I'm not that easy to shake off. The trouble with people in this village, they're too ready to stand back and let somebody else do the work, don't you think?'

'Yes, I suppose,' Kat replied automatically, her mind totally absorbed in what she was going to put on her CV. It was important she got it absolutely right. A job, a decent job, was her ticket out of this place. And she needed that ticket badly, before the people in this village drove her completely bonkers.

But how to word it, so it wouldn't sound as if she'd been fired from her last job? It's not like she had been fired, of course. More that she was a victim of the recession, of greedy bankers, of the radio station's falling ratings, all those things and more, according to Brad, the station manager. And, he'd added, it was hurting him more then it hurt her and that someone with her talent would find another job no trouble.

Which just went to show what he knew. After trying for four weeks to find another job in Bristol, and sinking further and further into debt, she'd finally had to admit defeat and come home to Millford Magna, where jobs were rarer than hens' teeth — and just about as appealing.

'So he said that he was doing his best and that he'd be advertising for staff as soon as he could get around to it.'

This time, it was Elsie Flintlock's strident voice that caught Kat's attention.

'Excuse me, Elsie. Who — '

'It's Mrs Flintlock to you.'

'Sorry. Mrs Flintlock. Did you say someone was looking for staff?' she asked. 'Only, as it happens, I'm looking for a job.'

'You've got a job,' Elsie sniffed. 'Not that you're making a very good fist of it.'

'Sorry. But who were you talking about?'

'Donald Wilson, at the pub. He needs a new barmaid. His wife's away on a cruise, you know. With her mother. So they say. But if you ask me, I reckon she's left him and who could blame her? He's got all the charisma of a wet week in Wigan. They had the most terrible row the week before she went and she called him a useless parasite and she should have listened to her mother and never married him in the first place. Course, she's the one with the money, you know, and he — '

'And you think he's looking for a new barmaid?' Kat said. 'Brilliant. I'll give him a call.'

'Well, I hope you make a better barmaid than hairdresser,' Elsie, who always had to have the last word, called after her.

But Kat didn't care. Any job, any job at all, had to be better than being up to her ears in perm lotion and gossip all day.

3

'Well, yes. I suppose I do need someone in the bar,' Donald Wilson said hesitantly. 'But it's only temporary. Joyce is away on a cruise with her mother. Won't be back for another two months.'

'Oh, that's fine by me,' Kat assured him. She hoped she'd get another job — a 'proper' job as she thought of it — way before Joyce Wilson came back from her cruise. 'And I can start immediately. Tonight if you like? I'm a hard worker and you won't regret taking me on, honest.'

He might not regret it, Kat thought later that evening as she stifled a yawn, but she did. Her feet ached, her back ached, her heart ached for the good old days when she had a proper job. She had this sinking feeling she'd jumped out of the frying pan of tedious local gossip in her mother's salon into the fire of even more tedious local gossip in the Black

Swan, better known to the locals as the Mucky Duck. But at least the smell of beer didn't make your eyes water, the way the perm lotion did. Even if all this enforced smiling was making her jaws ache.

'Just keep smiling at the customers, Katie,' Donald told her. 'That's the thing you need to remember.'

'I prefer to be known as Kat, if it's all the same with you.'

Donald shrugged and gave a weak smile. 'Yes, well, I prefer to be known as Don, but nobody ever calls me that. Everybody knows you as Katie, same as they all know me as Donald and that's the way it is, I'm afraid. Just keep smiling, even if some of them aren't exactly — ' He pulled a face. 'Well, just remember, the customer is always right. Oh, and don't stand chatting while there are customers waiting to be served. They don't like that either.'

But smiling and being nice while pulling pints of Ferrets Kneecaps Best Bitter was easier said than done when you're listening to a load of grumpy old men — and some of them not so old — moaning on about the government, England's chances in the Third Test and the date of the next recycling collection, at the same time fielding yet more questions about her career prospects and her love life.

'Couldn't keep away then, Katie? I knew you'd be back. You know what they say, don't you? You can take the girl out of Millford Magna but you can't take Millford Magna out of the girl.'

Kat glanced at the pint in her hand, then at Donald watching her and wondered if it would be worth going for the quickest sacking on record, if only to see the leery grin wiped off Gerald Crabshaw's face — or Councillor Crabshaw as he preferred — by a well-aimed pint of Ferrets. He'd been the ninth person that evening to make the 'Couldn't keep away then' comment and the joke, such as it was, was wearing a bit thin. Besides which, when he came to the bar, he'd lean across the counter and leer down her top every time she bent over.

Tomorrow night she'd wear a buttoned to the neck blouse. Preferably one with the words 'Yes, I am back and no, I didn't choose to be' emblazoned on it.

This wasn't the future she'd planned for herself when she'd left Millford Magna to go off to do her Media Studies course at college in Bristol four years ago. She'd honestly believed she would never be back here again. At least, only to visit. Not to live and work.

'So, what happened to that fancy job you had with that radio station?' Gerald asked. 'From the way your Dad talked, you were indispensable. Practically running the place.'

Kat glowered at her father, Terry, perched in his usual stool on the end of the bar nearest the dartboard. 'Well, you know how things are,' she said. 'The recession's hit everyone.'

No way was she going to admit to him, or anyone else in the village, that her so-called top job was in fact, as a lowly-paid general dogsbody who, far from being indispensable, was dispensed with quicker than Alan Sugar could say 'you're fired'.

'Do you know, Councillor, me and Cheryl, we're victims of the boomerang generation, that's what we are,' Terry boomed across the bar. 'This is what it's

15

like these days. You think your kids have left home and you just start making a nice bit of space for yourself when boom, back they come, like a flippin' boomerang. And bang, there goes my snooker table.'

This earned him a burst of laughter from his cronies, a pint from Gerald Crabshaw and another glare from Kat. Even Donald, not known for his joviality, smirked as he came up behind Kat, soft-footed as a cat and placed a pack of mixers on the floor behind her.

Gerald Crabshaw went across to join some of his cronies. He'd lived in the village all his life and was out of the Marjorie Hampton mould of fingers into everything — except he was there first. He was a District Councillor, Chairman of this, Treasurer of that, he saw himself as Mr Millford Magna. There wasn't a planning application submitted, a village hall booking made nor a complaint about the local bus service lodged that Councillor Crabshaw didn't have a hand in, or an opinion about.

'And what do you think Joyce is going to think about Donald employing pretty young barmaids while she's away?' Gerald asked the group around the bar. As he returned to his group on the table by the window, he gave Kat what he obviously imagined was a long suggestive wink. In fact, it just made him look as if he had a severe tic on one side of his face.

'Here, Donald, how's Joyce getting on with her cruise? Have you heard?' a man with heavily-tattooed arms and a fatuous grin asked.

Donald jumped, as he always did when someone spoke to him directly, like he was surprised someone had noticed him. He was, after all, a very easy man to overlook and, as he always crept about very quietly, he tended to appear unexpectedly. 'Joyce? Oh, right, Dave. No, I haven't heard from her. I don't expect to really.'

'Donald!' someone shouted, in a shrill tone that Basil Fawlty would have jumped to. Everyone in the bar laughed. Except Donald who gave a tight-lipped smile, like it was something he'd heard many times. Kat gave him a sympathetic grin but it was not returned. The Mucky Duck regulars were not known for the original-ity of their repartee, as she could testify to the number of times she'd heard the 'Couldn't keep away, then, Katie?' question that evening. Oh yes, and the 'Does Will Manning know you're back?' one. Not to mention the 'What have you done to your hair? Is that courtesy of rent-a-nest?' one.

On the other hand, over on Gerald Crabshaw's table the conversation suddenly sounded a lot more interesting.

Gerald's face was mottled red, his shrill angry voice cutting through the tedious chorus of those clustered around the bar.

'For heaven's sake, man,' he said to a browbeaten man sitting opposite him. 'What are you blathering on about? Everyone knows it was that wretched Marjorie Hampton who killed — '

'Here, Katie, don't stand there like a spare part.' Donald pointed to the crate of mixers. 'Unpack these and put them on that bottom shelf, will you? And we're running low on crisps.'

'It's Kat,' she said, without much hope of success. If that wasn't typical. The first time that evening there was a conversation that was remotely interesting and what happened? She missed it. Who was Marjorie Hampton supposed to have killed? She was a bit of a busybody — or, according to her mother, a lot of a busybody — and it was common knowledge that she and Gerald Crabshaw were at daggers drawn. But a murderer? Here in Millford Magna? Surely not.

By the time she'd put out the mixers, the conversation on Gerald's table had moved on to the riveting topic of the closure of rural post offices and an upcoming planning appeal. The browbeaten man's brow was looking more beaten than ever.

'What were you saying about Marjorie Hampton?' Her curiosity got the better of her when Gerald came up to the bar for a refill and another eyeful.

'Get me another packet of pistachios and I'll tell you, sweet Katie,' he smarmed, knowing she'd have to bend down to get them.

'So who's Marjorie Hampton supposed to have killed?' Kat asked, as with a move that would have impressed a limbo dancer, she managed to unhook the board containing packets of nuts without having to bend over.

'Interfering old baggage. That woman has been nothing but trouble since she moved in to the village. Sticking her nose into things that don't concern her.'

'But you said she'd killed somebody.'

Gerald laughed. 'Not someone, my dear, but something.' He took a long pull at his beer, looked round to make sure he was the centre of attention then puffed his chest out like he was practising for Prime Minister's Question Time.

'Marjorie Hampton,' he declared, 'killed the Farm Shop.'

A Farm Shop? Talk about a let-down. Kat thought he was talking about a nice juicy murder that would liven up the place a bit and give everyone something to talk about other than last night's Corrie and how things used to be back when men were men, women knew their place and the railway still went through the village.

'You've done it now,' Tattooed Dave muttered. 'Once you get old Gerald started on that, there's no stopping him. He'll be banging on for the next half hour about how this townie government is ruining rural life and all that rubbish. Isn't that right, Gerald?'

Gerald ignored him. 'If poor Sally Fleming was still alive it would break her heart to see what a sorry state her precious Farm Shop is in now, thanks to Marjorie Nose-into-everything Hampton.' He scowled and there was no sign of the smiling, genial man he'd been a few moments earlier. His small, too close together eyes were hard and cold, his mouth taut with barely suppressed anger. 'I tell you, that woman is going to poke her sticky beak into one pie too many one of these days and is going to come to a very unpleasant end, you mark my words. A very sticky end indeed.'

But before he could come out with any more words for everyone to mark, the front door crashed open and a large unkempt man stood swaying in the doorway. Conversation in the pub stopped as abruptly as if someone had thrown a switch.

'Evening John,' Donald said warily as

the man zig-zagged to the bar.

'Pint of best and a whisky chaser,' he slurred, and Kat could smell the whisky fumes on his breath from the other side of the bar.

'That'll be six pounds please.' As she handed him his drinks, she looked at him closely for the first time. She almost spilt the whisky as she recognised the wreck of a man who half stood, half leant at the bar, his eyes red-rimmed and bloodshot with several days' stubble on his face. His clothes looked like he'd slept in them for the last few weeks.

It was John Fleming, husband (or, rather, widower, Kat reminded herself with a twinge of sadness) of Sally and father of Will, the guy she'd always thought of as her brother and best mate when they were growing up.

Kat had last seen John Fleming about a year ago now. She'd been home for the weekend and had looked in on the farm to collect a pie from Sally and to tell Will what a prize idiot he'd been the night before. John was a big bear of a man, gentle, strong and softly-spoken, often teasing her about her aversion to mud and farmyard smells. At least, that was how he used to be.

'How — how are you, Mr Fleming?' she said, but he didn't answer. Gave no sign he'd even heard her, least of all recognised her. Instead, he tossed back the whisky, picked up his pint and stumbled off to a table in the far corner where he stayed, speaking only to order more drinks, until staggering out at about half past nine, ricocheting off the door frame as he did so.

Cheryl had told Kat how John had fallen apart since Sally's death from cancer four months ago but Kat had thought that was a bit of exaggeration on her mum's part. Sadly, it hadn't been.

Tomorrow, she promised herself, she'd go up and see Will. Even though he probably wouldn't want to see her. Not after the awful things she'd said to him the last time they met.

4

'The thing is, Mum,' Kat said the next morning, 'I don't know what to say to him. Particularly as I didn't go to Sally's funeral.'

'You were on holiday at the time. Even if you could have afforded it, there was no way you could have got back in time. Will understands that.' Cheryl took a spoonful of cereal and chewed it slowly. 'You're surely not going to have nothing but a chocolate bar for your breakfast. Eat some real food, for pity's sake.'

'What? Like you're eating? What is it?' She pointed at Cheryl's bowl of gloopy grey sludge that looked more like wallpaper paste. 'You're not on another diet, are you?'

'It's not a diet. It's a change of lifestyle. You remember Janet Thornton? Well, she came in to the salon a few weeks ago and I didn't recognise her. She's lost three stone on this. All you have to do is eat a couple of bowls of this every day and the rest of the time you can eat normally.'

'Eat normally?' Kat laughed. 'In all the time I've known you, you've never eaten normally. There was the grapefruit diet — and what about the one where you ate all that disgusting cabbage soup?'

Cheryl flushed. 'It's fine for you to laugh. You can eat whatever you like. But that's not necessarily a good thing. Like chocolate biscuits for breakfast. At least have a banana.'

'Sorry, but I'm really not hungry. And, by the look of you, you're not either.'

Cheryl sighed and pushed the dish away. 'It's no good. I can't eat this. Maybe I made a mistake in the recipe.' She took a biscuit. 'I'll start tomorrow. I've got a busy day ahead. Need to keep my strength up. Thank goodness Sandra will be back.'

Sandra was Cheryl's assistant who had been working for her for as long as Kat could remember. The years of standing up all day had taken a toll and she was, according to her, 'a martyr to her feet' and had spent the previous day travelling all the way to Bath to try some wonderful new chiropodist she'd heard of.

'So you won't need me today?' Kat asked.

'No. So you've got no excuse not to see Will. Just say you're sorry about his Mum. That's all you have to do. For goodness' sake, Katie. What's wrong with you? This is Will we're talking about. You used to be such good friends, remember?'

Remember? As if she was likely to forget. Chance would be a fine thing.

Ever since she'd come home, Cheryl had been nagging Kat to go up and see Will. But she'd kept putting it off. For one thing, when he'd met Ratface, the last time she'd brought him home, it had been a case of mutual hate at first sight. And now, Kat knew, Will would be unbearably smug about how he'd known it wouldn't last and how she must have been pretty desperate to have been taken in by such a poser. He wouldn't be able to resist it.

But the other reason, The Big One, was that she didn't know what to say to him. They'd had this terrible row the last time they'd met and it was going to be pretty difficult to say how truly sorry she was about his Mum (which she was: Sally was a really, really nice person and used to make the best meat and potato pies on the planet) while trying to forget that the last time they'd met, Will called Kat, among other things, a stuck up, selfish little cow and she'd called him, among other things, a pig-headed, carrot-crunching oik.

But she couldn't put it off any longer. She left Cheryl working her way through the chocolate biscuits, fished her bike out of the garden shed and cycled up the steep, narrow lane towards the Flemings' farm.

It felt strange to be going up there after all this time. When she was young she'd spent every spare moment at the farm, following Will around like a little duckling. They were both only children and he was the brother she'd never had. And like any other siblings, they squabbled and fought but usually made it up.

But when they fell out, a year ago now, it was for keeps.

All the way up the lane, she practiced what she was going to say. But she needn't have bothered because when she got there, the place was deserted. Not only were there no humans about, there were no animals either, apart from one of those crazy, wild-eyed collies that always slunk about the place and a load of black and white kittens skittering in and out of the barn doors like leaves in the wind.

But something else was different too and it took her a few minutes to work it out. It was the mud. Or rather, the lack of it. She'd put on her oldest shoes in the certain knowledge she'd be wading ankle-deep in goodness knows what just to get to the back door of the farm house. But instead the yard was so unnaturally clean, the concrete looked as if it had been bleached and there were weeds growing up through the cracks.

'Hello?' she called, but the only answer came from a dog inside the house who started barking and sent the other one in the yard into a frenzy, running around Kat like she was a stroppy old ewe he was determined to return to the flock.

'Tam. Enough.' A voice shouted and, to her relief, she saw Will emerge from one of the barns on the far side of the yard. He looked bigger than she remembered, his shoulders broader, his hair longer, but his eyes were the same disconcerting blue with the same long, sweeping eyelashes that she'd always told him were completely wasted on a bloke.

He stopped dead when he saw her and, instead of the welcoming grin she'd been sort of hoping for, he scowled.

'Oh, it's you. I heard you were back. What do you want?' he said.

'Well, not to be bowled over by the warmth of your welcome,' she retorted. 'Which, as it turns out, is just as well, isn't it?'

He scowled. Then his face relaxed, he raked his fingers through his hair and gave a half smile. 'Jeez, I'm sorry, Katie — '

'My name's Kat now as you very well know — ' she began but might as well have saved her breath.

'I'm sorry, Katie,' he said emphasising her name deliberately, which she knew he was doing just to annoy her. Just like he always did. Although this time she had the feeling he was doing it more out of habit than conviction. 'I'm a bit distracted, to be honest,' he went on, his hair sticking up all over the place, like a little boy who'd just been dragged out of bed. His eyes were indeed as blue as ever, but they were ringed by deep shadows, as if he'd not slept properly in weeks. 'It's Dad,' he went on. 'The stupid old fool didn't come home last night.'

'But I saw him last night. He was in the pub.'

'I know he was. But I've already phoned the pub. It was the first place I checked. Donald said he left about half past nine.'

'Yes, that would be about right.'

'Was he with anyone? More to the point, did he leave with anyone?'

Kat thought how he'd sat, alone, in the furthest, darkest corner of the bar. How each time he'd shambled up to the bar everyone else had done this kind of side-stepping shuffle, as they'd tried to edge away from him without making it too obvious. It was like some weird slow motion dance and all a bit sad but John had been too far gone to notice.

'He was on his own all night,' she said. 'Donald was chatting to him for a bit, but that was all. I don't think he even recognised me. And I'm pretty sure as far there was no one with him when he left.'

If there had been, she thought, they would have stopped him ricocheting off the door frame. But she didn't think Will needed to know that.

Will rubbed his face, his fingers rasping across several days growth of stubble. There was a bleak, hopeless look in his eyes, like he was lost and a bit scared. Kat had never seen him look like that before.

In all the years she'd known him, he'd always been so strong and in control. So sure of himself. A bit too much sometimes, she thought grimly as she remembered that last terrible row they'd had. But now, he looked like he didn't know who or where he was. He looked, too, like a man who had run out of options.

'Will — I'm — I'm so sorry I haven't

been in touch with you sooner.' Her tongue seemed to have stuck to the roof of her mouth as she stumbled over the inadequate words. 'And I'm so sorry about your Mum.'

'I got your card,' he said.

'I'm sorry I couldn't get back for the funeral. It must have been tough for you.'

'Tough?' He looked up, his eyes meeting hers for the first time. He looked so angry, she backed away.

'Look, I'm sorry. That was a stupid thing to say.' Her words tumbled over themselves as she floundered about, not knowing what to say next. 'I knew I'd say the wrong thing. I shouldn't have come. I can see that now. I'm just making things worse, idiot that I am. I just wanted to say I'm sorry. About your Mum. And everything. That's all.'

She began to walk away but he called after her.

'Katie? Oh, all right then, Kat. Please wait.' He caught up with her before she reached the gate, putting his hand on her arm to stop her. 'Come back, please. I'm sorry. I shouldn't have barked at you like that. As for you not being at the funeral, your Mum explained. And, to be honest, I didn't even notice. Look, come in and have coffee and we'll catch up. I've got ten minutes before I have to go and take some feed up to the stock in Top Meadow.'

He strode across the yard, with Kat half running as she always did when she tried to keep up with him.

'But what about your dad? I thought you were on your way out to look for him?' Her heart lurched. 'Do you think he's had an accident? Have you spoken to the police? You don't think he's — ?'

'I think he's sleeping it off somewhere. He's done it before. I've already checked the obvious places. The only question is — where?'

'What's happened to him?' she asked and could have bitten her tongue off for asking such a stupid question. It wasn't like she needed a degree in psychology to work it out for herself.

He opened the back door and, with a sharp command, quietened both dogs.

'You must have seen the state of him

last night,' he said, bleakly.

'He — was a bit, er— ' She hesitated for a moment as she wondered if she was about to break some barmaid code of conduct but what the heck? Will was, or at least he used to be, a mate. 'He was already in a bit of a state when he came in, reeking of whisky. He stayed for about an hour, downed several pints with whisky chasers, then staggered out, bouncing off the porch wall as he did so. And you're saying he never made it home?'

Will shook his head. 'I don't know where else to try. I've been from here to the pub and all round the village and back, expecting to find him sleeping it off under a hedge somewhere, like he was the last time. I've also been down to the pond and walked as far as I could up the river. Shouting. Calling. Nothing. He seems to be on one permanent bender at the moment. He could be lying dead in a ditch for all I know — except I've looked in all the ditches.'

5

'Are you sure you shouldn't contact the police, then?' Kat asked, her voice edgy with panic. 'I mean, anything could have happened to him. And if you're that worried — '

'Nothing will have happened to him,' he said. 'I'm sorry. I didn't mean to worry you. I'm just tired, that's all. Didn't get much sleep last night and then up at the crack of dawn this morning. Dad will turn up. He always does. When he sobers up. Which he'll do for a couple of days, then something will set him off and it starts all over again.'

'Was there something in particular 'set him off', as you put it, this time?'

'Damn right there was. He'd had a bit of a run-in with Marjorie Hampton and I've never seen him so angry. I told him not to take any notice, that she was nothing more than an interfering busybody, but I'm not sure he heard me. He

35

just grabbed the whisky bottle and stomped off to his room with it. Then, about half an hour later, I heard the front door slam and realised he'd gone out. The whisky bottle was empty and I reckoned he'd gone to the pub.'

She frowned and shook her head. 'It's hard to believe, isn't it? He was always such a careful, controlled man. In all the years I've known him I've never seen him the worst for drink, not even that time at the Harvest Supper when someone was a bit heavy-handed with the fruit punch and we all ended up tipsy, even your Mum. But not your Dad. He was the only sober one in the whole village.'

Will gave a little half smile at the memory. His smile faded abruptly. 'Not any more, he's not,' he said bleakly.

'How long has he been like this?'

'Ever since the funeral. He started that night, after everyone had gone home, and he's been drinking steadily ever since. It's like he's got a flippin' death wish, the stupid old fool.'

'He's grieving, Will,' she said gently.

'And I'm not?' Those three quietly

spoken words told her more plainly than anything else could have done the depths of his grief and once again she felt guilty that she hadn't been there for him, her oldest friend.

'Of course you are.' Her voice was husky as she squeezed his hand. 'Now, what about that coffee you promised me?'

She followed him into the kitchen where she'd spent so much of her childhood, bottle-feeding orphan lambs in front of the Aga or sitting at the big scrubbed table trying to talk Will into doing her maths homework for her. Her mother used to complain that she spent more time at Will's house than her own. But then, Will's house didn't smell of perm lotions or hum with the constant buzz of gossip.

The outside of the farmhouse was the same as ever, even down to the Victoria Plum tree that Sally had trained up the front, one branch as tantalisingly close as ever to the upstairs landing window where she and Will would risk life, limb and Sally's anger every Autumn as they reached for the luscious purple red fruits.

Nothing had changed at the farm. Except for the unnaturally clean yard.

Inside, however, was something else. The kitchen, once so warm and welcoming and always smelling of furniture polish and baking, was freezing and Kat didn't want to think about what it smelt of. Even the big cream range that Sally had polished and shone until it gleamed, had given up and gone out. Sally would have been devastated by the state of it.

As they went in, a black and white cat shot off the table, where it had been eating the remains of what Kat imagined was a microwave curry of some sort, judging by the lurid colour. And even the cat, it seemed, had wisely decided to pass on the unappetising lump of sweaty cheese and the grey-blue slices of mouldy bread that spilled across the cluttered table.

'Jeez, what a tip.' The words were out before she could stop them. 'Oh Will, I'm sorry. I didn't mean — '

'Forget it.' Will switched on the electric kettle, then rummaged among the teetering pile of crockery in the sink for mugs.

'Dad's as much use as a chocolate teapot these days so I'm running the farm single handed. It's all I can do to look after the livestock. There's precious little time left for housework at the end of my day.'

Nor for eating properly, either, she thought, her eyes soft with pity. But this time she kept her thoughts to herself. Instead, more from a desire to change the subject than anything else, she asked: 'Where are the cows? I've never seen the yard so clean.'

'I'm so glad something meets with your approval.' A hint of the teasing smile she remembered so well tugged the corner of his mouth as he rinsed out two mugs. 'We got out of dairy. There's no money in milk production anymore so we sold the herd a while ago now. Just as well, as things turned out. If I was having to cope with twice-daily milking on my own, on top of everything else, I'd have given up. We've only got beef cattle now — and the sheep, of course. They're the reason Mum started the Farm Shop in the first place.'

It was more than a year since she'd been in Sally's Farm Shop. Back before

Sally became ill with the cancer that had overwhelmed her with such sudden, shocking swiftness. Kat and Ratface had been on a rare visit home and Cheryl had more or less insisted they go up to the shop to collect some pies that Sally had put by for them.

Kat wasn't keen. The last thing she wanted to do that morning was bump into Will again. They'd done so in the Mucky Duck the previous night and to say that Ratface and Will hadn't hit it off would be like saying Tom and Jerry weren't exactly best buddies. It wasn't helped, of course, by the way Ratface kept saying 'ooh arr' in a poor and extremely annoying imitation of a Somerset accent and making jokes about local yokels which were about as funny as a party political broadcast.

But she needn't have worried. Will wasn't around that day. Just Sally, as pleased as ever to see her.

The Farm Shop was in a small stone building that used to be the Cheese Store back in the days when cheese was made on farms and not in factories. Sally had stocked the shop with freezers full of home-reared lamb, chiller cabinets stuffed with home-made pies, and cakes and shelves that groaned under the weight of jars of her pickles and jams.

She was a small, compact woman with enough energy to power the National Grid. Always busy, always had some new project on the go, always full of life and laughter. It hurt to think of all that brightness snuffed out. Sally Fleming, Kat thought as she swallowed hard, was one of the good guys. It was so unfair.

She blinked away the tears that were making her eyes smart, accepted the mug of coffee Will handed her and pulled a face. 'No milk?' she asked.

He picked up a carton from among the debris on the table, sniffed it and tossed it into an overflowing bin. 'Not unless you fancy taking a bucket to one of them up in Top Meadow,' he grinned, knowing how jumpy she got anywhere near the rear end of a cow.

'Gerald Crabshaw was ranting on about Marjorie Hampton in the pub last night,' she said, changing the subject quickly. 'I thought at first he'd said she'd killed someone and that we had a nice juicy murder on our hands in Millford Magna, which would have livened the place up a bit, wouldn't it? But he was talking about the Farm Shop. He shut up quickly enough when your Dad came in though.'

Will put a third spoonful of sugar into his coffee and stirred it vigorously. 'That's just Gerald, trying to put one over on Marjorie as usual,' he said. 'He's had a down on her ever since he lost his license for drink driving after one of Donald's late night lock-ins. He's convinced she was the one who tipped the police off. Apparently, she'd had a go at him only a couple of days before about driving his Porsche when he'd had one too many.'

'But in what way could she have been responsible for the — ' She shied away from Gerald Crabshaw's melodramatic turn of phrase. ' — the difficulties of the Farm Shop? I assume it does have difficulties?'

'It's all but closed, to be honest. Which is a shame because things were going really well until Mum got ill. Remember old Mr Taylor at the Post Office?'

She nodded, took a sip of her coffee, then wished she hadn't as she tried to suppress a shudder. 'Dad told me he'd retired, sold the shop to a developer who promptly turned it into a holiday cottage.'

'Couldn't blame the poor old chap for selling up although there were lots around here who did. Nobody wanted to take the Post Office on as a going concern. But Mum worried about how the old folk were going to collect their pensions and wanted to save them the hassle of catching the bus into town. So she persuaded the Post Office to set up what they call an Outreach Service in the Farm Shop.'

'And that worked, didn't it? I remember Dad telling me about it.'

'It worked really well to start with. In fact, it had such a good effect on trade that Mum started buying in a few bits and pieces of groceries. Tea, coffee, baked beans, that sort of stuff. Then, Marjorie Hampton decided it was too far for the old folk to come all the way up here to collect their pensions and that Mum's prices were too high. Do you want some more coffee, by the way? See? I remembered how you drink it by the gallon.'

'No, I'm fine,' she said quickly, wishing there was a convenient plant she could tip it into. 'I'm trying to cut down on caffeine. So what did Marjorie Hampton do?'

'She organised a minibus to take them all into town, and of course, the supermarket. Got some local bigwig to sponsor it as well, so it didn't cost them a penny. And, so of course, they jumped at it. Then the Post Office had one of their regular culls of rural Post Offices and the one at the Farm Shop had to go.'

'So that's what Gerald Crabshaw was on about. How awful. It must have been a desperate blow after all your Mum's hard work.'

'Not really.' Will took a sip of coffee, pulled a face and added yet another spoonful of sugar. 'She'd become ill by then and it was all Dad and I could do to keep the farm ticking over, without taking on the Farm Shop as well. And when she died, neither of us had the inclination to do anything about it. Dad because he can't see his way out of a bottle at the moment, and me because — well, the truth is, I can't bear to go in there, knowing Mum's not going to come bustling in any moment . . . .'

His voice trailed away and there was such unbearable sadness in his eyes that Kat forgot about the stupid row and remembered they were mates. She put her cup down and moved across to take the chair next to his.

'It's OK,' she said, putting her hand over his. 'Your Mum would understand. She wouldn't want you to beat yourself up about it.'

Will sat there for ages, staring at nothing. His hand felt work-roughened and cool beneath hers and gradually she became aware of the silence, the sort she hadn't heard for years, broken only by the ticking of the clock on the old dresser and the distant bleating of sheep.

'I've heard Gerald and his nonsense,' Will said eventually. 'But, you know, it wasn't Marjorie Hampton who killed the

Farm Shop. More the fact that we're only a twenty-minute drive from the nearest supermarket.'

'You might not blame her. But perhaps your Dad does? Do you think that's what they rowed about yesterday?'

'I shouldn't think so. He doesn't seem to give a toss about anything on the farm. Now,' he went on with a false brightness that didn't fool Kat for a nanosecond, 'there's bound to be a nice leg of lamb in one of the freezers. Do you think your Mum and Dad would like it?'

'No, that's all right. I don't want you going in there on my account.'

'I've got to do it sometime. In fact, I thought, well, now you're here. Will — ' He hesitated, and held out his hand. 'Will you come with me, Katie? Please?'

Kat's heart went out to him and once again, she cursed herself for staying away from him for so long. 'Of course I will. But only if you promise that you and your Dad will come and eat it with us,' she said as she followed him out of the house, down through the yard and towards the old Cheese Store.

'You're on,' he said, taking out a bunch of keys out of his pocket. 'I haven't had a roast dinner since I don't know when and I think even Dad might be persuaded. He likes nothing better than a nice leg of lamb. It might — hello, what's been going on here?'

'What's the matter?'

'The door's already unlocked.' He swore softly. 'I didn't think to check in here. That's probably as far as the old fool could stagger last night. What's the betting we find him stretched out in here?'

They did indeed find John Fleming stretched out in there. They also found a nice leg or two. But they didn't belong to a lamb.

Instead, they were sticking out of one of the freezers, clad in thick grey tights and wearing what Kat's mum would have called a 'nice sensible pair of shoes'.

6

'Wh-what's-the-matter?' John Fleming struggled to his feet and shambled towards them, his eyes bloodshot, his breath more toxic than anything that ever wafted out of his farmyard. 'Can't a fellow have a kip in peace now?'

'Is this your idea of a sick joke, Dad?' Will asked, pointing at the open freezer.

'A joke?' Kat let go of Will's hand, which until then she'd been holding so tightly it had left nail imprints. Of course. It was a joke. Stupid of her to have been so freaked out. Just a sick joke.

'Look, Mr Fleming,' she laughed, light-headed with relief as she walked towards the open freezer. 'Someone's stuck a pair of dummy's legs in here and for a moment, I thought — '

'Katie. No.' Will pulled her back but it was too late.

She'd got close enough to see that the legs didn't belong to a dummy but to a woman with a nice tight perm and a Midnight Hyacinth rinse. Only there wasn't much left of Cheryl's handiwork. Just this sickening mess where the back of poor Marjorie Hampton's head should have been.

Will's arm was tight around her shoulders, pressing her into his chest and holding her so tight she could hardly breathe. Somewhere, someone was making a low, moaning noise. It took Kat several seconds to realise it was her.

John Fleming did not move. He stood, as if frozen, staring at the freezer, his jaw slack.

Will's face, as he looked at his Dad over Kat's head, was the colour of cold porridge. 'What the hell have you done?' he asked in a hoarse whisper.

'Me?' John Fleming looked bewildered then angry, as he looked from the body to his son, then back to the body again. 'Hells teeth! You think I did that?'

'Then what's she doing here? I know she came to see you yesterday afternoon. I heard the two of you having a row. What was that about?'

'Interfering old baggage,' John snapped, the colour coming back into his face. 'Going on about the overgrown footpath across Middle Field. Said it was a disgrace — and so was I. Told me how I should pull myself together. That Sally would be ashamed of me.'

'She's not wrong there,' Will growled.

John grunted. 'That's as maybe. But it's not her place to go sticking her oar in. So I told her to clear off and mind her own damn business. And, furthermore, I said, if I caught her on my land again, I'd get my shotgun — '

'Dad.' There was a warning note in Will's voice. 'I'm going to call the police. When they get here, don't you dare say things like that, otherwise they'll think you did it.'

'Of course I didn't do it,' he roared. 'Yes, we had words and yes, I told her to get the hell off my land. But she did just that.'

'What time was that?' Kat asked.

'What?' He looked at her as if she'd just asked him to prove Einstein's Theory of Relativity.

'Do you happen to know what time Marjorie left here?' she said. 'Only it might be important. And the police are sure to ask you.'

'No, of course I don't,' he said sharply, then checked himself. 'Wait a minute, yes, I do, as it happens. I heard the kids coming out of the school. You know what a noise they make. In fact, the old baggage had a grumble about it, you know how she goes on. Young people today and all that. So that must have been half past three, or so. Wouldn't you say?'

'And you're sure about that, Dad, are you? You're sure you stood here at half past three and watched her walk away?'

'No. I didn't exactly watch her. I — ' He pushed his hand through his thinning hair. 'To be honest, I don't really recall. It's all a bit of a blur after that. I'm pretty sure I went into the barn and . . . .'

'And everything else is a blur,' Will finished as John's voice trailed away. 'Well, the police are going to really love that story, aren't they? Are you sure you didn't come in here?'

'What about that, Katie? My own son

thinking I could do something like that.'
His anger died abruptly and, with a pleading look in his eyes, he added: 'I suppose she is dead, isn't she?'

She nodded and closed her eyes in a futile attempt to shut out the image that would surely haunt her for the rest of her life.

'I'll just — ' He took off his jacket and approached the freezer but Will caught him and yanked him back.

'What are you doing? For God's sake, don't touch anything. The police — '

'I was just going to cover her up,' he said, in a dazed voice. 'She wouldn't want people to see her like that, would she?'

Kat touched his arm. 'I don't think it makes any difference to her now, Mr Fleming,' she said gently. 'Come on, let's get out of here, shall we?'

* * *

The last time Kat had seen so many police together at any one time had been the Glastonbury Festival. Only this was no fun-filled, rain-soaked weekend. No 'nice juicy murder' either, Kat thought with a guilty start as she remembered what she'd so stupidly wished for the previous day. Murder wasn't nice. Or juicy. Nor some entertaining, intellectual puzzle to while away a couple of hours in front of the television.

Murder was shocking. Disorientating. Sordid and deeply scary. It took your lovely joined-up world and shattered it into millions of tiny, disconnected pieces.

Looking back on it later, the first few hours following the discovery of Marjorie Hampton's body were a complete blur. The only thing Kat remembered with any clarity was sitting in the cold, dust-laden sitting room that obviously hadn't been used since the day of Sally's funeral. Being asked the same questions, over and over again. And each time she answered, the same sickening picture flashed into her mind and stayed there, even when she shut her eyes. And each time the horror was as fresh as if she was seeing it for the first time.

Eventually, she assumed, the police must have realised she couldn't tell them anything else and said she could go. She went out across the yard to collect her bike, trying not to look at the entrance to the Farm Shop, now cordoned off with blue and white police tape that fluttered in the chilly morning breeze.

She stepped back as a police car drove past, with John Fleming hunched in the far corner of the back seat, a policeman by his side. Will stood by the yard gate, ashen-faced, gripping the top bar of the gate as he watched them drive away. The dog, as always, was by his side.

She walked up to him, the dog nuzzling her hand as she did so, his nose cold against her skin. 'What's happening? Where are they taking your Dad?'

'Yeovil Police Station.' He sounded dazed, like he'd been roughly woken from a deep sleep.

'But why? They're surely not going to charge him? He'll need a lift home once they realise they've made a mistake. Come on, Will. Get the car out and we'll go after him.'

'There's no point. According to the sergeant over there, he's just 'helping them with their enquiries'. Not that he's in any fit state to help anyone, least of all himself, he's that hungover, the silly old fool.'

'But that's ridiculous. Why can't he help them with their enquiries right here? Why drag him all the way to Yeovil?'

He shrugged. 'Search me. He wasn't helping himself, that's for sure. I tried to get him to shut up but he went on and on about how he and Marjorie had had words and he'd told her to push off. Even called her an interfering old baggage, would you believe? Right there, in front of that stony-faced sergeant. He — he said — ' He gripped the gate rail tighter than ever and turned to face her. 'You know what they found in the shop, near her body, don't you?'

'No.' The look on his face warned her that it was bad. Very bad.

'They found his shotgun.'

'But it hadn't been fired, had it?'

'They're taking it away for forensic examination. He said he'd been using it to shoot rabbits yesterday.'

'And had he?'

'Yes, I think so. I can't swear to it but I'm pretty sure I heard him, up there in the top meadow. But it's one of those sounds you hear so often that you don't take any notice. So even that didn't help him.'

'So they think Marjorie was shot, do they?'

'How would I know? They don't tell you anything. Just ask the same questions over and over.'

'Don't they just.'

'And Dad — he was getting more and more wound up, the more they asked.' He turned his face away and looked down at his hand, still gripping the top of the gate, his knuckles white. 'I was just waiting for him to come out and say how he'd threatened her with his shotgun if she came back. For all I know, he'd probably done so already. They're going to pin this on him, Katie. I know it,' he said in a low, hopeless voice.

'Of course they won't. Because he didn't do it,' she said with complete conviction.

'Yeah, right. And they never get things

wrong, do they? Innocent people never get convicted. Because he is innocent, isn't he?' He dragged his hand down across his face and his eyes, when he looked up, were full of fear. And a hint of doubt. 'You know, Marjorie Hampton really got under his skin the other day. Lecturing him about how he should pull himself together, how ashamed Mum would be of the way he's behaving. He was beside himself with fury. I've never seen him like that before.'

'Will, don't go there.' She placed her hand over his and squeezed tightly. 'Marjorie Hampton is — was an interfering old busybody who had no right to speak to your Dad, or anyone else, like that. Of course he got mad with her. Anyone would have done.'

'Yeah, I suppose you're right.' Still the doubt — and the fear — shadowed his eyes.

'Now you listen to me, William Fleming,' she said fiercely. 'Your Dad's one of the gentlest, kindest people I know. Remember how he showed me how to take care of the orphan lambs? And taught me to ride that bad-tempered little pony of yours, when all you did was laugh at me and call me Scaredy Cat? And how he cried, along with us, when Blue died?'

'He loved that old dog, didn't he?' A smile flickered across Will's face as he reached down and fondled the black and white collie, who whimpered and pressed closer into his legs.

'Like I say, he's a big softy. He could never — ' She swallowed hard as that dreadful image filled her head again.

'And in the pub last night,' he said harshly, his eyes bleak. 'Was he a big softy then, do you reckon?'

'Well, no,' she said slowly. 'He was — '

'Morose. Drunk. Anti-social. Not exactly the man you remembered, I'll bet. Not the same man who cried over a dead dog.'

Kat was forced to admit she hadn't even recognised John when he'd first stumbled into the bar last night. 'Even so, underneath it all, he is the same man. He'd never do something like that. No matter how drunk, or angry, he was.'

'I hope to God you're right. But if he didn't, then who did?'

'How would I know? I just know it's not your Dad,' She took his hand. 'Look, come on down to our house. At least you'll get a decent cup of coffee there. Don't stay here on your own.'

He shook his head. 'No. I'm going to stay here and see if I can get hold of a solicitor. Then I've got to go up and sort out the animals. I was on my way up there before — Before. Thanks for everything. For being there. I appreciate it. I'll let you know, about Dad.'

He turned to go into the house, the dog and Kat both following him.

'It's OK,' he said. 'I'm fine. I don't need babysitting. Honest.'

'You might be fine. Your kitchen, on the other hand, is disgusting. I've got an hour before my lunchtime shift at the pub. You go and do what you have to do and I'll clean up. It's not going to help anyone if you go down with salmonella poisoning.'

'You, doing some housework? Now that's a first. This I must see,' he said with a quick grin. And in that moment, in spite of the grimness of the day, Kat's spirits gave a little lift. It was so good to feel back on the old easy terms with Will again. It was just a pity it had taken such a tragedy to have brought them back together.

She punched him on the shoulder. 'This is a one-off, you do realise that, don't you? It's just that I don't ever want to taste anything as awful as that coffee you made me just now ever again. It was gross.'

'You didn't complain at the time.'

'That's because I was being polite, you moron.'

He laughed. 'Now I know I've wandered into a parallel universe. Katie Call-Me-Kat Latcham, not only doing the washing up but being too polite to complain? She'll be wearing a frilly apron and rubber gloves next.'

'In your dreams, boy. And if you don't get out of here, I'll have you wiping up.' She started lifting the crockery out of the sink. 'I've just had a thought. Someone's bound to have seen Marjorie Hampton yesterday after she'd been up to see your Dad. I should be finished in the pub in time to catch the school run. Some of the young mums may well have seen her after they'd had their set-to, which would put him in the clear, wouldn't it?'

It was a long shot. But, like the washing up, it was good to be doing something.

7

Kat glanced anxiously at her watch for the tenth time in as many minutes.

'Are we holding you up?' Elsie Flintlock said sharply. 'Only the way you're hopping about, you're giving me heartburn. Me and Olive have come in here for a quiet, pensioner's lunch and we don't expect to be hurried out, like we were in the way. This isn't one of your fast food, eat all you can as quick as you can, places. Respect, young lady. That's what you need to learn. Respect for your elders. We fought a war for you lot, you know. Just you remember that.'

Kat bit back a retort. There was no point in arguing with Elsie Flintlock. You could never win. Her keen blue eyes missed nothing and her acid tongue could have stripped varnish. Donald grumbled that the pair of them always stayed longer if the weather was cold, to save on their heating bills at home.

She was the leading light in the Millford Magna Grumble and Gossip Group — or, to give it its correct title, Millford Magna Young Wives Group. Not that any of their members were under sixty-five. It was just that there hadn't been a vicar in the last twenty years with the courage to change the name.

But, if anyone knew who was doing what, where and to whom, Elsie Flintlock was that person. What she didn't know about the goings-on in the village probably hadn't happened.

'No, of course I'm not in a rush, Mrs Flintlock. You take all the time you need,' Kat said, collecting the empty glasses and putting them on the bar. 'I was just hoping to catch my friend, Jules, on her way to pick the kids up from school. But it doesn't matter. I'll catch up with her later.'

'Jules? What sort of name is that?' Elsie frowned. 'I suppose you mean Ted Harper's youngest, Juliet. The one you used to be really friendly with until you dropped her for your trendy new friends in Bristol.'

'I didn't drop her,' Kat protested. 'She got married and I moved thirty miles away, that's all. We've kept in touch.'

Not strictly true. Jules had got pregnant with Kylie at about the same time Kat started college and they didn't have much in common any more. Over the last five years, they'd exchanged the odd email and followed each other on Facebook but not much else. But Elsie didn't need to know that.

'I've heard she's in the family way again,' Elsie said, with a shake of her head. 'That useless husband of hers doesn't earn enough to keep himself in shoe leather least of all a growing family. And they're already bursting at the seams in that little shoebox of theirs. Olive here was only saying just now, how they're going to fit another in — '

'I want to ask her about John Fleming. Or rather, if she or any of the other mums saw Marjorie Hampton on Tuesday afternoon after she'd been up to the farm to see him.'

That got Elsie's attention. Or at least diverted it away from Jules and Ed. Her little blue eyes glinted as she drained her glass and handed it to Kat. 'I'll have another half of Ferrets please and Olive will have an orange juice. And you can tell that skinflint boss of yours, he can be done under the trades description act for calling that soggy mess we've just eaten a steak and mushroom pie. Not a single mushroom and if that was steak, then I'm Victoria Beckham.'

Kat smothered a smile. Anyone less like Victoria Beckham than Elsie Flintlock was hard to imagine. 'Do you want me to pass your complaint on to Donald?'

'No point. So, what were you saying about John Fleming? I hear he's been charged with Marjorie Hampton's murder and that it was you who found her headless body.'

'Not headless,' Kat said with a shudder. 'And John Fleming hasn't been charged with anything.'

'Not yet he hasn't but it's only a matter of time. Not that he was the only one around here with a motive. That Marjorie Hampton has got up more noses than grass pollen in the hayfever season. I'm surprised there wasn't a queue lining up to do for the nosy old parker.'

Settling down for a long, cosy chat with Elsie Flintlock was the last thing Kat wanted. On the other hand, the old gossip might be able to tell her something.

'Anyone in particular?' she asked.

'She's upset practically everyone in the village at some time or another,' Elsie said. 'Even told poor old Olive here that she shouldn't let her cat do his business in other people's gardens. Isn't that right, Olive?'

Kat didn't think it likely that Olive Shrewton, who always reminded her of one of those grey herons who hung about on the river banks, was capable of killing Marjorie. But then, neither was John Fleming.

'So when was the last time either of you saw Marjorie?' she asked.

'I saw her at your Mum's,' Elsie said, while Olive shook her head. 'Having her hair done. As you know, seeing as you were there at the time, trying to have me catch my death of cold by pouring freezing water down my neck. Even though I was good enough to tell you about the job going here.' She looked at Kat critically. 'You know, you're not a very good advert for Cheryl's salon and I've told her as much on several occasions. If you're going to work in there on a regular basis, you're going to have to smarten yourself up, young lady. Have you combed your hair this morning?'

'Of course I have. It's supposed to be like this. It's the fashion. And I'm not going to be working in the salon any more. I was only covering for Sandra while she was away having her bunions done, or whatever.' Kat cleared away the empty plates and resisted the urge to point out that the pies couldn't have been that bad seeing as both plates looked as if they'd been licked clean. 'Did you happen to know where Marjorie was going, after she'd had her hair done?'

'How would I know? You were the one she was talking to, not me. Weren't you listening?'

'Well, yes. Sort of. She was going on about footpaths and something about how she was going to stand up to someone once and for all. But it was quite noisy in the salon that morning and I didn't catch all she said.'

'Did she now?' Elsie became fully alert, like a bloodhound scenting its quarry. 'Now, who do you reckon she was meaning?'

'I don't know. Except, I don't think she meant John Fleming, because — '

'I think it's about time you were off home, Katie,' Donald said, coming up so quietly behind her, it made her jump. He had a habit of doing that and it was starting to freak Kat out. It was as if he had a hidden camera that sent him an alarm every time she stopped to talk to anyone.

But she didn't have to be told to go twice. Particularly as it was obvious that information gathering was strictly a one-way process as far as Elsie Flintlock was concerned.

Kat grabbed her coat and hurried out, determined to catch Jules on her way to school.

* * *

As Kat left the pub, she was just in time to see Jules, ahead of her, with a couple of other mums on their way up to the school, which was set a little way out from the centre of the village, up the narrow high-banked lane that led eventually to the Flemings farm. A cold wind was blowing and she pulled her coat tighter around here, then hurried to catch up the girl she'd been friendly with ever since primary school.

'Jules!' she called.

Jules turned round, a beaming smile on her face as she recognised her. 'Katie, I heard you were back. Hey, you're looking good, girl. I love your hair. It's really cool.'

'Thanks. Although I was asked, just now, if I'd combed it this morning. And told I was a pretty poor advert for Mum's salon.'

Jules laughed. 'It's great to see you. Here, I've just heard about Marjorie Hampton. And that it was you who found her body. Terrible, isn't it?'

'Shocking. And it's Kat,' she said automatically.

'Sorry. I keep forgetting. You told me the last time you were home.' Jules pulled her collar up against the wind that was funnelling up the narrow lane. 'But you know how folk around here hate change. You're little Katie Latcham. Always have been. Always will be. Even when you become a rich and famous radio presenter.'

'In my dreams. You know I got made redundant from the radio station, do you?'

'Yeah, I heard. That's tough. So, apart from that, how are things with you, Kat? I hear you and that guy — what was his name? — split.'

'Nick,' Kat said shortly. 'Also known as Ratface. And is there anyone in this village who doesn't know about my love life? Or lack of it?'

'Shouldn't think so,' Jules grinned. 'Once Elsie Flintlock gets hold of a piece of goss, you may as well take out a front page advert and announce it to the world.'

'Tell me about it,' Kat sighed. 'She told me lunchtime you were in the family way, as she put it, again. Is that right?'

Kat was sorry to see the smile vanish abruptly from her friend's face. She hadn't meant to upset her and, for the first time, she noticed how tired and worn Jules looked. Her hair, which was usually so bright and glossy, was scraped back into a lank ponytail and her clothes looked as if she had just grabbed the nearest thing to hand, which was so unlike her. Of the two of them, Jules had always been the sharp dresser.

'Old witch,' Jules muttered. 'How the hell did she know that? I haven't even told Eddie yet. He's going to be over the moon — I don't think. Another baby was definitely not part of the plans. Not now things are getting a bit easier, with our Kylie starting school. And then, I had this job, which I had to pack in because I've been getting the most terrible morning sickness that lasts morning, noon and night and he wasn't prepared to give me any more time off.'

'God, I'm sorry, Jules. That's tough,' Kat said sympathetically. 'This place is the pits for knowing everyone's business, isn't it? I'd forgotten just how bad it can be.'

'Look, I can't stand here talking, much as I'd like to. Kylie goes mental if I'm not there when she comes out of school. She only started in September and hasn't really settled yet. Walk with me?'

'Sure.'

'I hear Marjorie Hampton was decapitated. That her head was in one freezer and the rest of her in the other. Is that true?'

'No.' Kat didn't want to think about Marjorie's blue cauliflower head as it had been the last time she saw it. But, as far as she could tell, it had still been firmly attached to her body. 'I saw her, you know. Yesterday afternoon. I was helping Mum in the salon because Sandra had gone to Bath to see a chiropodist — '

'God, is she still working for your Mum? I thought she'd have been pensioned off years ago?'

'Still there. Do you remember how we used to call her Mrs Overall, after that Julie Walters character?'

They giggled and for the first time

since coming back to Millford Magna, Kat felt a sense of connection. It was so good to see Jules again and have a laugh over old times. Good, too, to forget, if only for a fleeting moment, Marjorie Hampton's brutal murder which had filled her mind ever since the grim discovery.

'So, go on,' Jules prompted. 'You say you saw Marjorie in the salon?'

'She came in to have a perm. She said she was going up to see John Fleming later. Something about a footpath closure.'

'And you reckon that's when he murdered her?' Jules's pale tired face lit up.

'No, of course I don't. John Fleming didn't do it. No way. For pity's sake, Jules.'

'That's not what I heard. Not what the police think either, by all account.'

'Then the police are wrong,' Kat said with conviction. 'It has been known, you know. Look at that time they thought your Eddie had been receiving stolen copper cables.'

'That was a mistake. The dumbo bought them in good faith from a dodgy mate. I'm always telling him he should pick his mates more carefully.'

'Exactly. A mistake. The police were wrong about Eddie and they're wrong about John Fleming.'

'But if John didn't do it, who did?'

'I don't know.' An image of Will's shocked face as he watched his father being driven away in a police car swam into her mind. Followed by another of John Fleming's face, as white and shocked as his son's. How must he be feeling now, locked up in a police cell? He was a man of the outdoors, never comfortable in confined spaces. It must surely be freaking him out. 'But I intend to find out,' she added.

'Hah!' Jules laughed. 'Hark at you. Millford Magna's Miss Marple.'

Kat turned, part way up the hill that led to the school and looked back on the village, stretched out below them. It looked so quiet — dead even, the sort of place where nothing much happened. And yet, somewhere down there was someone who thought he — or she, of course — had just got away with murder.

'No, seriously, though, Jules,' she said. 'Did you see Marjorie up here Tuesday afternoon?'

'No. But I was late picking Kylie up. I had to go into town and the wretched bus was late coming back. It had to go all round the lanes as there'd been a nasty crash and the road was closed most of the afternoon. That's why I don't want to be late today. She'd got in a terrible state, convinced herself that I was never coming back and Miss Davenport, her teacher, now has me marked down as 'A Bad Mother'.'

'What about any of the other mums?' Kat asked. 'Did they see Marjorie?'

'I don't know,' Jules said. 'You'll have to ask them.'

They'd arrived at the school by this time and Kat spent several minutes going from one group of mums to the next. But nobody, it seemed, had seen Marjorie Hampton coming back after John Fleming had told her to get off his land although a few had seen her on the way up. One had even spoken to her.

'Interfering old cow,' she said. 'Only told me my little Skye shouldn't be eating a lolly. That it would rot her teeth. Like it was any of her business.'

'So that would have been about half past three, would it?' Kat asked.

She shook her head. 'More like quarter past. I was early. I always am. First to arrive, last to go, that's me.'

Quarter past three. That meant Marjorie would have reached the farm at about twenty past. How long does it take to have a row and be ordered off? One thing was sure, John wouldn't have invited her in for a cup of tea and a biscuit.

'I didn't see her come back down though,' the young mum went on. 'And I was here for ages, waiting for my Marlon who'd lost his reading book and had to stay behind until he found it. He'd lose his head if it wasn't screwed on, that one. Just like his Dad. It must have been closer to four when we finally got away.'

Kat frowned. That didn't make sense. The only way to and from the Flemings' farm was via the lane that led past the

76

school. If Marjorie had left John at the time he said she had, then she'd have had to come along the lane. And someone would have seen her.

Which either meant John had got the time wrong and she'd left much later. Or she hadn't come back at all. That John had lost his temper, which he admitted he had, and —

And nothing. She shook her head, cross with herself for letting her thoughts skitter off in that direction.

John Fleming was innocent. Of course he was. And she was going to prove it.

8

After she left Jules, Kat went on up the hill to the farm to see if Will had any news. She'd already decided not to tell him about how she'd drawn a blank trying to find someone who would admit to having seen Marjorie Hampton after she left the farm.

And yet, of course, if John Fleming was to be believed, somebody had.

But the yard was deserted, apart from the kittens who'd been playing with the blue and white police tape that still fluttered around the entrance to the farm shop. They skittered back to the safety of the barn at her approach and the fact that there were no dogs barking hysterically as she entered the yard told her that Will must be out on the farm somewhere.

She knocked long and hard on the farmhouse door, hoping John might be back and would open it, but there was no reply. She took out her phone to call Will but put it away again. There was no point. Will's mobile was the least mobile phone in the world and spent most of its time on the dresser in the farmhouse kitchen. She scribbled a note asking him to let her know what was happening and if there was anything she could do, pushed it through the letterbox and went back home to spend the rest of the afternoon trawling the internet for jobs and sending out applications.

It was a soul-destroying task, knowing that most, if not all of them, wouldn't even bother to answer, least of all take it any further, and it was almost a relief when it was time for her evening shift in the pub, even if it did mean another evening of mind-numbing boredom like the previous night had been.

But she'd reckoned without the power of a gruesome event like a murder to pull a community together. Or, as was more likely, to bring out the ghoul in everyone. The Mucky Duck was heaving like it was Christmas Eve, as people came along to see if they could find out any more, other than the stark statement that had been on the early evening local news.

Talk about one man's tragedy being another man's good fortune; Donald had a smile on his face a mile wide. He'd even put roast lamb — a rare treat, usually reserved for special occasions — on the Specials Menu and was doing a roaring trade, while his beer sales went through the roof.

Everyone, it seemed, apart from Kat and Will, was convinced of John Fleming's guilt and came out with one story after another about his heavy drinking and the anger that had been eating him alive ever since Sally died. And, as the evening went on and the beer flowed, the stories and speculation grew more lurid and outrageous that Kat's jaw ached with the effort of biting back the desire to scream at them all to shut up.

She was asked so many times if it was true she'd found the body — always with that same, barely contained frisson of excitement — that by the end of the evening she was wishing they'd go back to asking her about her love life, as they'd been doing the night before.

'Face it, love,' Cheryl said next morning when Kat grumbled about how it seemed as if the whole village had the poor man tried and convicted. 'John's not the man you knew anymore.'

'Nobody changes that much. Not to do something as awful as that. This is John Fleming we're talking about, remember? The man who taught me to ride that bad-tempered little pony of Will's. The man who fixed my bike so that Dad wouldn't know I'd ridden it into the village pond and buckled the wheel.'

'Did you? I didn't know that.'

'You weren't supposed to.' Kat prised the lid off the biscuit tin and peered inside. 'And where are my chocolate biscuits? There was half a packet left in here. What happened to this wonderful new diet?'

'It was making me depressed,' Cheryl said, then smiled. 'Besides, your Dad says he prefers me with a few curves. Says it gives him something to hang on to — '

'Whoa! Way too much information,'

Kat cut in hastily. 'Seriously, Mum, you don't really believe John could have done such a terrible thing, do you?'

Cheryl's face clouded and her voice softened. 'Not the John we used to know, no,' she said as she placed a gentle hand on Kat's arm. 'You're quite right. He was a lovely, gentle and very kind man. But he's changed, love. It's as if when Sally died, he died too and this bad-tempered stranger took his place. I'm not saying he meant to kill poor Marjorie. More likely he struck out wildly in one of his drunken rages. You have to remember, grief can do terrible things to a person, and John — well, like I said, he's not the man he used to be anymore.'

'I still don't believe it,' Kat said. 'It's so awful, not being able to do anything to help.'

'But you are doing something. You've made it up with Will and that can only be a good thing. And didn't you say you'd cleared up the kitchen for them? That would have helped. I'll pop a casserole in the oven this morning and you can take it up to them after you finish at the pub lunchtime. And, no, before you ask, it's not one of my special diet recipes. It's a good old-fashioned lamb hotpot, made the way Sally used to make it.'

But Kat thought it would take more than lamb hotpot to take the haunted look out of Will's eyes.

★   ★   ★

As soon as her lunchtime shift at the pub was over Kat collected the casserole from her mum and went straight up to the farm to see if Will had any news.

As she got there, he was crossing the yard, the deranged Tam pooling around his feet as always, like a mid-day shadow.

'Hey, Will? Why didn't you answer my note?' she called.

He turned at the sound of her voice. 'What note?' He looked blank. He also looked as if he hadn't got much sleep last night.

'The one I put through your front door yesterday.'

He shook his head. 'You have been away a long time, haven't you? You know

83

we never use the front door. So what did your note say?'

'Only to let me know if you've any news. About your dad.'

'Get down, Tam,' Will said, as the dog began to dance around Kat's feet.

'I expect he can smell this. It's a hotpot. Mum made it for you — and your dad.' She handed him the bag containing the casserole.

'Thanks. That was good of her. Tell her I appreciate it. But it looks like I'll be the only one eating it.'

'Your Dad's not back then? Have you heard anything?'

'Yes, I've heard.' His voice was razor-edged with bitterness. 'It's not good. He's still helping them with their enquiries. Oh yes, and he's refusing a solicitor. Says he doesn't need one and is ready to confess to killing Marjorie.'

'Oh no.' The news was as bad as it could be. But still Kat refused to believe John Fleming had murdered Marjorie. 'Did he say why? Or how? Or why he dumped her body in the freezer? It certainly wasn't to hide it. The whole thing makes no sense.'

'He doesn't remember. He just said he supposed he must have done it when he was drunk. They haven't charged him yet but it's only a matter of time. They've collected all the evidence they need from the Farm Shop, or the crime scene as they call it.'

'And what about his shotgun? Was Marjorie shot?'

'Apparently not. It seems she was hit over the back of the head with the proverbial blunt instrument.'

Kat gulped back a wave of nausea at the memory. 'But, surely, that's good news for your dad.'

'Not if they find the blunt instrument with his fingerprints all over it.'

'Which they have failed to do. Obviously. Otherwise they'd still be crawling all over the place, which they're not. And your dad would have been charged with murder. Which he hasn't.'

'Not yet he hasn't. Although the place is still sealed off. And they've been through the house with a fine-tooth comb. They were very suspicious at the sight of recent attempts to clean the kitchen up. Spent forever testing that.'

Kat's heart lurched. 'But that was me. I'll tell them it was me. Jeez, I hope I haven't made things worse for him.'

'Shouldn't think so. They could hardly be a lot worse, could they?'

'But Will, you surely don't think he could have done it?'

'Of course I don't. But there's plenty around here who do — and who won't hesitate to tell the police so. Dad's rubbed quite a few people up the wrong way in the last few months.'

Kat decided against telling him about some of the stories that were flying around the bar last night. 'But he said Marjorie left when he told her to, remember? That it was about half past three because he heard the school children. Somebody must have seen her going back down the lane. I've already asked the mums on the school run and although several saw her on her way up, no one saw her come back. So tonight I'll make a point of asking everyone in the pub. It was a bit difficult to do last night because we were really busy and Donald was hanging around all the time.'

'According to Dad, his 'discussion' with Marjorie lasted only a few minutes. If, as he says, she'd gone straight back she'd have been seen by at least half a dozen mums waiting by the school gate.'

'But what about her neighbours? Surely they'd have seen her coming and going Tuesday afternoon?'

Will shook his head. 'It's all holiday cottages down that end of the village now and at this time of year they're empty. Face it, Kat. If anyone had seen Marjorie that afternoon, they'd have come forward by now.'

Kat sighed. He was right, of course. But at least he'd called her Kat which was progress of a sort. 'Nevertheless, it won't hurt to ask around, will it?'

True to her word, Kat asked everyone she served that night if they'd seen Marjorie on Tuesday and got the same negative answer. Nobody, it appeared, had seen her after she'd stopped to lecture that young mum about the state of her child's teeth.

Nobody, of course, except John Fleming.

Donald's glares every time Kat asked were going from stormy to hurricane.

'I pay you to work, not stand around gossiping all day,' he hissed at one point. 'If you want to do that, maybe you'd be better off working in your mother's salon.'

So when Gerald Crabshaw came in, she waited until Donald had gone down the cellar to change a barrel and beckoned Gerald to come closer.

'You brighten up the place no end, sweet Katie,' he said with his usual leery grin as he leaned across the bar. 'You're certainly easier on the eye than old Donald and I must say that's a lovely top you're almost wearing. What was it before? A handkerchief?'

She yanked at the hem of her favourite sparkly blue top and wished she'd borrowed one of her mum's cover-all tee shirts instead. She'd chosen it because it had a high neck and hadn't given a thought about how it also flashed a bit of bare midriff every time she moved, something that had never bothered her until that moment. The way Gerald Crabshaw looked at her, his piggy little eyes gleaming like he was famished and she was the main course, made her flesh crawl.

Still, she reminded herself, this was not the time for the snarky put-down, much as she would like to. Instead, she forced herself to give a little giggle, as if he'd just said something incredibly witty, as she handed him his pint. 'Did you see Marjorie Hampton any time after four o'clock on Tuesday afternoon?' she asked.

'Me? Of course I didn't. Why on earth would I?' His smile vanished as abruptly as if she'd slapped him in the face. 'Fancy yourself as an amateur sleuth, do you? With me as suspect number one? Here, Donald, I've just been interrogated,' he called out as Donald appeared, soft-footed as ever, behind her. 'Young Katie reckons it was me and not poor mad John Fleming who did for Marjorie Hampton.'

Although he laughed when he said it, Kat could see from the spots of colour high on his cheeks that he didn't find it terribly funny. And Donald looked like he was about to blow a head gasket.

'Don't take it personally, Councillor,

and have that one on the house,' he said in a low voice that was not meant to be overheard, in case it started a stampede of people demanding drinks on the house because they too had been 'interrogated'. It was a clear indication of how rattled he was as Donald was well known for his aversion to handing out free anything, particularly drinks. 'Our Miss Marple here has been asking everyone the same question. She even had the cheek to ask me if I had an alibi for Tuesday afternoon, and of course I told her that you and I had a site meeting about possible new playing fields for the village out on that bit of waste ground out on the bypass, didn't we? And that it took the best part of the afternoon.'

It wasn't true, of course. Kat had asked him nothing of the sort. But she'd already annoyed him enough for one night so she figured, if she wanted to keep her job, it would be best to let it go.

But she needn't have bothered. Later that night, as she went to get her coat, he called her back into the bar.

'Don't come in tomorrow,' he said.

'Oh? But I thought my day off was Monday? Tomorrow's Saturday.'

'I am well aware of what day of the week it is,' he said coldly and Kat had a bad, bad feeling she wasn't going to like what was coming next.

She was not wrong.

'Here's what I owe you for the hours you worked.' His brisk, decisive voice was a million miles away from his usual soft, hesitant tones. 'Less, of course, the cost of Gerald's pint.'

She could tell from the way he pointed his finger at her that he was a fan of The Apprentice. This was his Alan Sugar moment and he looked like he was milking it for all he was worth.

'You're fired,' he said.

9

'You're firing me? But why?' Donald wasn't known for his sense of fun, but this was his idea of a joke, surely? She'd only had the job for four days. Her dad was going to go ballistic. And her mother was going to insist she spent more time in the salon.

'Well, not exactly fired,' he said. 'More a case of being made redundant. I told you the job was only temporary, didn't I?'

'You did. But there's temporary and there's downright unfair.' Her head was reeling from the shock. 'You said your wife wasn't due back from her cruise for a couple of months.'

'Yes, but you weren't replacing my wife, but my other barmaid who's been unwell but is now fit for work again.'

'But you can't do that — '

He cleared his throat and at least had the grace to look uncomfortable. 'I'm sorry but I'm afraid I can. To be honest, you're not really what I'd call barmaid material. People come in here for a quiet drink, you know, not to be given the third degree by some smarty-pants college kid playing Cluedo. I'm sorry, but I've got to act on my customers' complaints.'

Sorry? From where Kat was standing, he looked about as sorry as a fox in a henhouse. She grabbed her coat and stomped off, knowing that as soon as she told her Mum, Cheryl would have her back in Chez Cheryl's before you could say highlights, seeing as Sandra's feet were still 'giving her gyp' as she put it, in spite of that very expensive visit to a tip-top chiropodist.

She wouldn't mind betting it was that smarmy Gerald Crabshaw who'd made the complaint about her. He'd been livid when she'd asked him if he'd seen Marjorie the day she died, which was, on reflection, a pretty over-the-top reaction to such an innocuous question.

Was he, then, the person Marjorie had said she was going to have it out with, once and for all? The person, she said, who was not going to get away with it?

And was he, then, the person Marjorie had met after John Fleming had ordered her off his land?

As she walked home, along the village's deserted main street, she tried again to remember what Marjorie had said that day in the salon. It beat thinking about what her mum and dad were going to say when they found out she was out of a job. Again.

Marjorie had wittered away the entire time Kat was rinsing her hair but Kat had been thinking about what she was going to put on her job applications and wasn't really paying much attention, apart from adding the occasional 'No? Really? And what did you do then?' Talk about making a drama out of a crisis. It was one thing after another with Marjorie, like everything and everyone set out deliberately to annoy her. If it wasn't the shocking state of the footpaths or corruption in the Planning Department it was the latest power struggle in the Floral Art Society.

'He's not getting away with it,' Kat could remember her saying. 'He'll find I'm a force to be reckoned with once I've got my dander up. It's got to stop. And I'm going to make sure it does. It's about time someone in this village had the courage to stand up for what is right.'

Who had got Marjorie's dander up, whatever that was? And what was it that had to stop?

Was there any point repeating all this to the police? She hadn't a clue who Marjorie had been talking about but the police would simply assume it was John Fleming. The last thing Kat wanted was to make things even worse for the poor guy. She'd done enough damage cleaning up the kitchen and the police hadn't really wanted to know when she'd spoken to them that morning to tell them so. They'd merely said her comments had been noted.

But she knew Marjorie hadn't been talking about John Fleming. She'd already had a go about him and had moved on. Idiot that she was, why, oh why, hadn't she listened more carefully? Her Mum was always going on at her for having her head in the clouds and not listening. And for once, her Mum was right.

Although there was no way she'd ever tell her that.

★ ★ ★

Her parents took the news of her dismissal from the Mucky Duck with surprising enthusiasm. Her dad's reaction was understandable. Even though she'd taken on board the little lecture Donald had given her on a barmaid's need for discretion, particularly in a small gossipy place like Millford Magna, and hadn't said a word to anyone about who was drinking what, how much and with whom, her dad had never been keen on her working there. He'd said it was because it was a waste of her talents and training — and he wasn't wrong there. But the real reason was, Kat suspected, that he'd been worrying about Cheryl finding out exactly how many pints of Ferrets actually made up what he called 'just a couple'.

Her mother's reaction, however, was just plain weird.

'Oh, thank goodness for that,' she said.

'What's to be thankful for? Being fired four days into a job?' Kat demanded.

'Well, no, that's not good, I grant you. But I'm sure Donald must have had his reasons,' Cheryl said. 'I've always found him a very reasonable man, if a bit on the drippy side. No, I meant from my point of view, it couldn't have happened at a better time. You can help me in the salon. To be honest, I was wondering how I was going to manage with poor Sandra still laid up with her bunion. I did think of asking young Millie Chapman, but she's not what you'd call reliable.'

'And I am?' Kat said. 'That isn't what you said when Elsie Flintlock accused me of pouring cold water down her neck and giving her the new-monials again.'

'Yes, well, hopefully there won't be a repeat of that.'

'But I was going to spend the day doing job applications.'

'One more day won't make any difference. Saturday's always busy and I'm fully booked all day. Our first appointment is at half past eight so you'd better get off to bed as you've an early start in the morning.'

Kate sighed. Could things get any worse? Not only was she back, living at home with her parents. No job, no boyfriend, no money, no prospects. She was even being told by her mother what time to go to bed.

* * *

It was the first time she'd ever put in a full day in her mother's salon and by the time she took her so called lunch break at half past three, she was bushed. Her feet ached, her back ached, her fingers ached, her brain ached, while the smell of perm lotion and hair spray leached out of every pore.

In between listening to people moaning about their husbands, in-laws, children and how there's nothing worth watching on the telly any more, she managed to slip in the odd question about possible sightings of Marjorie Hampton on Tuesday. But she got the same answer she'd received in the pub. No one had seen Marjorie after four o'clock. And neither, it seemed, did anyone have the slightest idea who she might have been talking about that day. It could be anyone as most people in Millford Magna had got Marjorie Hampton's 'dander' up at one time or another, even their mild, inoffensive vicar who wanted nothing more than a quiet life, tending his begonias.

But the general consensus was that it was probably John Fleming, as one of her latest campaigns had been about the state of the local footpaths, in particular a blocked one somewhere on his land.

Kat finished her sandwich and was just trying to summon up the energy to go back into the salon, when her phone went. It was Will.

'I thought you'd like to know, I've just been down to Yeovil and brought Dad back.'

'That's brilliant,' she said. 'I knew they'd realise he's innocent eventually.'

'He's not off the hook yet,' Will said. 'It's more a question of they didn't have sufficient evidence to charge him so they had to let him go. For now. Told him not to leave the area though.'

'So he obviously thought better of that phoney confession?'

'Yeah. The solicitor I found for him finally made the old fool see sense.'

'And how is he?'

'Sober. And subdued. Keeps apologising. Will you be in the pub this evening? I thought I might drop in for a quick one.'

'You must be the only person in the village who hasn't heard, Will. Donald fired me last night.'

'The devil he did. Why?'

She decided not to tell him it was because she'd been upsetting the customers by asking questions about Marjorie Hampton. 'He said I wasn't barmaid material but the truth of the matter is, I was only a stand-in while his regular barmaid was off sick. How do you like that?'

'Tough. You must be seriously cheesed off.'

'Tell me about it. Especially as Mum's had me working in the salon all day. It was pretty dire working in the Mucky Duck, but this place is worse.'

'OK, so how about we go into Dintscombe this evening? There are new people in the Queen's Arms and they're really making a go of it. They have live music on a Saturday night and it's that dreary folksy stuff you like.'

'I'm sorry.' She rubbed her aching back. 'I've been slaving away since the crack of dawn and I've another couple of hours to go here in the torture chamber, by which time I'll be fit for nothing, except collapsing in the bath and then falling asleep in front of the TV. Another time, eh?'

'Sure. Let me know if you change your mind.'

'OK, but don't hold your breath. Oh and Will?'

'What?'

'I'm glad we're mates again. I — I really missed you, you know.'

There was a tiny pause. 'Yeah. I missed you too,' he said quietly, his voice suddenly croaky. 'Enjoy your bath.'

She ended the call and was about to put her phone away when it rang again and a number she didn't recognise came up.

'Is that Katie Latcham?' He had one of

those soft Irish accents that could make a shopping list sound like a poem. 'It's Sean Ryan here, from the Dintscombe Chronicle.'

Her heart did a triple somersault. The Dintscombe Chronicle was the local paper and was among the first she'd sent her CV to when she came home. Dintscombe was a small market town five miles from Millford Magna and the Chronicle was a typical small town newspaper, more interested in advertising revenue than news. She'd gone there to do her work experience when she was at school and had enjoyed it well enough. It wasn't exactly top of her wish list but it sure beat working in the salon and could well be a useful stepping stone.

She held the phone closer to her ear and hoped he wouldn't hear the frantic beating of her heart. No need to let him know just how desperate she was.

'Thanks for contacting me,' she said. 'I'm available for interview at any time and — '

'Well, we can do it right here and now, over the phone,' he said. 'And then if we want a picture — '

'Sorry?' Something about the way he spoke rang alarm bells. 'You mean you're not ringing about my job application?'

'I'm afraid not. That's not my department. I'm on the news desk and I'm doing a follow-up on the murder in your village this week. Thought I'd do a bit of a background piece. I understand it was you who found the body?'

She frowned. 'How did you get my number?'

'Ah well, I did what I always do when I want to find out what's going on in a place. I went to the local pub. It was a bit quiet lunchtime but I did have a drink with a very nice fellow called Terry, who says he's your — '

'Dad,' Kat said with weary resignation. Was it possible, she wondered, to divorce your parents, particularly ones who gave your mobile phone number to strange guys who just happened to buy them a pint or two?

'He said you found the body, is that right?'

'Yes, but I'd rather not talk about it.' To

be honest, she'd rather not think about it, either. Rather not wake up in the middle of the night, getting flashbacks. Seeing poor Marjorie's legs sticking out of the freezer over and over again. She'd rather not. But she did.

'Ah well, it's up to you,' he said carelessly. 'As a matter of interest, what job were you applying for? I mean, should I be worried now, do you think?'

'Oh no. Nothing like that. It was no job in particular. I just sent in my CV on the off-chance,' she said as she launched into the spiel she'd written and rehearsed so many times. 'I — I was employed by a commercial radio station in Bristol until a couple of months ago and enjoyed the journalism side of it so much, I thought I'd go for a change of direction. I did a journalism module as part of my Media Studies course and really enjoyed it. I just sent in my CV to your paper on the off-chance.'

'I see. Well, Katie — '

'I prefer to be known as Kat, if you don't mind. Kat Latcham is the name I am known by professionally.'

'Is that a fact? Well, Kat, do you fancy meeting up some time and I can maybe give you the heads-up about possible openings for you in the Chronicle?'

'Brilliant. That's really kind of you, Mr Ryan.'

'It's Sean. That's the name I'm known by . . . professionally.'

Kat laughed. 'Are you making fun of me, Mr Ryan?'

'Wouldn't dream of it, Kat Latcham. So, come on, now. How about tonight? There are new people in the Queen's Arms and they have live music on a Saturday night. We could meet up for a quick drink and a chat. Shall we say eight o'clock? I usually sit on the table near the window. You can't miss me. I'll be holding a copy of the Chronicle.'

It wasn't until she put her phone away that Kat realised she was no longer tired. The thought that maybe, just maybe, she could get a job on the Chronicle put all thoughts of a quiet night in front of the television clean out of her head.

The rest of the afternoon zipped by as she went through in her mind which of her work she would put in her portfolio to take along to show him. Then, there was the vexing question of what to wear.

⋆ ⋆ ⋆

She saw him the moment she entered the crowded pub. He was, as he'd said, sitting at the table by the window, a copy of the Dintscombe Chronicle propped up in front of him. He was younger than she'd imagined, in his early thirties probably, with dark hair that curled slightly over the collar of his snowy white shirt.

He was eye-wateringly, drop-dead gorgeous and when he smiled as she approached him, it was like the sun had come out.

'Mr Ryan, I presume?' she grinned.

'Good to meet you, Kat Latcham.' His handshake was cool and firm. 'Now, what can I get you to drink?'

'Mineral water, please.' She wasn't driving. Her dad had given her a lift in and she was getting a taxi back. But she wanted to keep a clear head.

She took the seat opposite him and he made his way to the bar. As she did so,

106

she became aware of someone watching her. She turned round and saw Will not just watching, but glaring at her.

'Will. I thought you didn't like dreary folksy music?'

'And I thought you were planning a night in front of the TV,' he snapped. 'All you had to do was say no, Katie. You didn't have to make up phoney excuses.'

'But it wasn't like that — ' she began. But it was too late. He'd already stormed out of the pub.

10

'Sorry. Did I interrupt something?' Sean asked as he returned with the drinks.

'No. Just a mate of mine being a total moron as usual.' Kat reached into her bag and took out the folder containing some of her work. 'I've brought some of my stuff for you to have a look at. It's mostly pieces I did for the radio station plus a few random bits I thought you might be interested in.'

'I'd rather find out a little bit more about you, Kat Latcham,' he said. 'You're working in your mother's hairdressing salon, I understand. I'll bet you hear all the local gossip there, don't you?'

'Tell me about it,' Kat said. 'My ears are still ringing.'

'And what are the jungle drums saying about Marjorie Hampton?'

Kat's hand stilled, the glass half way to her lips. 'I thought I told you I didn't want to talk about the murder. Is that why you asked me here, hoping I'd change my mind? This is all about you getting a scoop, isn't it? Nothing to do with a job with the Chronicle.' She gathered up her folder and stuffed it back into her bag, her cheeks flaming. Of all the naive birdbrains. What was she thinking of? If she hurried, she could catch Will and snag a lift back with him.

'Exclusive,' he said quietly.

'What?'

'We say exclusive, not scoop. If you're going to become a journo, Kat Latcham, at least get the terminology right. Now, sit down and we'll start again. Yes, I would like to know about how you found poor Marjorie Hampton but no, I did not ask you here tonight for that sole purpose.'

'So what was your purpose?'

'It's Saturday night. The music's good here and they do a decent pint, unlike that rubbish they serve in your local. I fancied a few drinks in the company of a gorgeous girl. Nothing more. Nothing less. Except, of course, a chat about job prospects with the Chronicle.'

Gorgeous? Did he say gorgeous? Kat's

ruffled feathers slowly began to unruffle. 'Yeah, right,' she laughed. She'd heard all about silver-tongued Irishmen who could charm the birds from the trees. 'We've never met before. For all you knew, I could have had a face like a horse and be covered in spots.'

A face like a horse. Of all the stupid things to say. The one thing guaranteed to bring Marjorie Hampton's horse-like features back to the forefront of her mind.

'Ah, but you see, I checked you out of Facebook. A good journalist always does his homework. Number one rule. Now, are you sure you wouldn't like something stronger?'

She smiled as the knot of tension that had been coiled inside her for days now slowly began to unwind. 'A good journalist should also know not to believe everything he reads on Facebook. And a Pinot Grigio would be lovely. Thanks.'

Two glasses later and the knot had completely unravelled. Sean was good company and she was astonished by how much they had in common, including their love of what Will called 'dreary folksy music' and their attempts to escape from small country villages.

'Poor you,' Sean said when she told him why she'd come back to Millford Magna. 'I know how I'd feel if I had to go back to the little village near Cork where I come from. You can't change your socks there without everyone talking about it and coming to the conclusion that you're part of an international sock smuggling ring.'

'And are you?' she laughed.

'Ah well, now that would be telling, wouldn't it?'

'So how did you end up in Dintscombe? It's not exactly a great metropolis,' she said. 'Five pubs, a kebab shop and a night-club that opens when the owner is sober enough to remember to open the doors.'

'Ah no, but I don't intend staying at the Chronicle all my life. It's just a stepping stone. That's why I want to make a good fist of this murder story.' His face became serious and there was a faraway look in his eyes. 'It's the biggest thing to happen around here since forever and I need to make the most of it. This could be the Big One.'

'But I — '

He reached across and placed his fingers on her mouth. Gossamer light and cool against her lips. She only had to open her mouth, ever so slightly and — oh Lord, what was she doing? And, more to the point, what was he saying? She'd completely lost track of the conversation.

' — And I would hate to spoil a lovely evening by upsetting you again. So, there will be no more talk of murder, ok?'

'Oh, but I don't mind talking about it. Not now. In fact, in some ways it would be a relief. It's just the actual finding her that I don't want to dwell on. I think that will haunt me for the rest of my life.' She shuddered. Time to think about something else. 'John Fleming didn't do it, you know. Although I seem to be the only person in the entire village who thinks so. Apart from his son Will, of course.'

'And would that be the total moron — your words, not mine — who stormed out earlier? That was John Fleming's boy?'

'That was Will, yes. You know John was

released without charge this morning, don't you?'

He nodded. 'That's because they'd held him for thirty-six hours. After that time they have no choice. They have to either charge him or release him. And obviously they've not got enough evidence to charge him.'

'Or they've found evidence against someone else,' Kat said. 'Because he didn't do it, Sean. I know it as surely as I know my own name. He says Marjorie left him at half past three and I believe him. It's just that I've asked almost everyone in the village now and nobody saw her after she went up to the farm.'

'Or nobody admits to seeing her,' Sean said quietly. 'But, if John Fleming is to be believed, then somebody did. Somebody has lied to you, Kat. The question is, who?'

'Gerald Crabshaw!'

'As in Councillor Gerald Crabshaw? The next leader of Dintscombe District Council who exchanges funny hand-shakes with my editor? What makes you say that?'

'Because he was the one who got me fired. Donald as good as admitted it. I'd been asking everyone who came into the bar if they'd seen Marjorie that afternoon and Gerald went bonkers at me. Said I'd been accusing him of 'doing for her' as he put it, which I hadn't. An hour later, Donald fired me saying customers had been complaining.'

'Really? Now that is interesting. As a matter of fact, I've been hearing things about Councillor Crabshaw.'

'What sort of things?'

He shrugged. 'Just local rumours. Unsubstantiated, of course. And nothing I could print. But even so, I've heard whispers about him. But I have to be careful because, like I said, he's a mate of my editor.'

'And that means he can get away with — ' She stopped.

'With murder? Was that what you were going to say? You think he murdered Marjorie?'

'Well, why not? It was no secret that they absolutely hated each other. And only the other night, he was going on

114

about how she was going to come to a sticky end one day. And, believe me, he never said a truer word. Her end was as sticky as you could get. And no, before you ask, I don't want to talk about it.'

The idea of poor Marjorie's undignified end being splashed across the front pages of a newspaper for people to exclaim over across the cornflakes was horrible.

'No pressure. Would you like another drink?'

'No thanks. To be honest, I'm absolutely whacked. Mum's had me working in the salon since the crack of dawn and all I want now is to go home and sleep for a week.'

'Some other time then?'

Her heart lifted. 'I'd like that very much.'

'I would offer to drive you home, but — ' He held up his drink.

'That's ok. Dad says he'll come and pick me up when I'm ready. He's trying to make it up to me after I had a go at him about giving out my mobile number to strange men in the pub today.'

He laughed. 'Look, if you'd like to leave that folder of work with me, I'll take a look at it,' he said. 'I'll be honest, there are no staff jobs going on the paper at the moment. The movement of staff tends to be the other way round, with falling circulation, loss of advertising revenue and threats of redundancy hanging over our heads. But there may be some chances for freelance work, if you're up for it? It doesn't pay a fortune but — '

'I'm up for it,' she said quickly.

'Great. I'll get back to you on that. Oh, and Kat?'

'Yes?' His smile was doing funny things to her knees again.

'I'm really glad your dad gave me your number, so I am.'

So was she — but there was no way she was telling her dad that.

* * *

Kat glared at her phone in frustration. Why did Will bother having a phone if the wretched thing was never switched on? She wanted to explain about last night

116

— and also to ask why he'd stormed off the way he did.

There was nothing for it. She'd have to go up and see him. But as she left the house she heard someone call her name. She turned to see Jules coming down the street towards her.

'Hi. You're looking very smart this morning,' Kat said. 'Going somewhere nice?'

'Hardly.' Jules pulled a face. 'I'm going to work. Donald phoned Saturday morning and asked me if I wanted my job back. And with the baby and everything, I could hardly say no. Eddie's on short time and things are pretty tight.'

'Donald? You mean you're working in the pub?'

'Always did catch on quick, didn't you?' Jules grinned.

'But that was my job — I didn't realise . . . ' She didn't know why, but the thought of Jules being the reason Donald had sacked her didn't sit very comfortably. 'Donald, the rat, said I was just cover while his regular barmaid was off sick.'

'You were working in the Mucky Duck?'

Jules had that look of studied innocence on her face that Kat remembered only too well. It had got her out of trouble many times. 'When?'

Kat was going to challenge her — after all, nothing happened in this village without everyone else knowing, least of all someone who worked in the pub. Instead, she shrugged. She hadn't liked working there anyway and if there was half a chance of some work with the Chronicle then it was all for the best. 'Actually, it was probably the quickest sacking on record. I started work Wednesday evening and he sacked me Friday night. Said I didn't have what it took to be a barmaid.'

'The rat. He sacked me last Monday when I phoned in to say I was sick again. Which was nothing but the truth, even though I told him I had an appointment with the doctor next day and was hoping he'd give me something to help. Which he did and I'm beginning to feel half human again now that I can keep my food down. My Mum reckons I'm carrying a boy this time and I was certainly never like this with my Kylie.'

'So how come you're working for him again?'

'He rang yesterday and offered me my job back.'

'That was once he'd given me my marching orders. You should have told him what to do with his job, Jules. I would have.'

'Yes, well, we don't all have your good fortune, do we?' Jules said sharply, her pale cheeks scarlet, her eyes hot and angry. 'No wonder people round here don't think of you as Kat. You're still little Katie Latcham, running home to mummy and daddy when the going gets tough. And yes, I suppose you would have told Dippy Donald where to stick his lousy job. You can afford to, seeing as your mum has fixed a job in her salon for you, even though young Millie Chapman really needed that job.'

'I — I didn't know.' Kat looked at her old friend. How stupid she'd been to think they could just pick up their easy-going friendship where they'd left off. Was that why Will had been so angry with her last night? Did he, too, think she'd taken their friendship for granted, thinking she could just move back home and everything and everyone would slip back into where they'd been before she left?

'And that's another thing,' Jules went on. 'I might as well get it all off my chest, once and for all. I've been wanting to say this for ages, even though Eddie tells me it's none of my business. It's about you and Will.'

'Me and Will?' Kat echoed, blankly.

'You really hurt him, you know. The last time you were home with Lover Boy. I've never seen Will so cut up.'

'You mean, the night after he and Nick nearly had a set-to in the bar? I should damn well think so. He — well, they both behaved like a pair of oafs. I don't know what came over him.'

'Don't you? Then you're blind. For pity's sake, couldn't you see? He might as well have had it stamped on his forehead. The guy was eaten up with jealousy.'

'Will? Don't be ridiculous. Why would he be jealous?'

'He's fancied you for ever. You must have realised. Why else do you think he used to run around after you like a little puppy dog? For pity's sake, girl, grow up. My Kylie shows more sense than you sometimes. Now, if you'll excuse me, I've got to go to work.'

Will fancied her? What was Jules on? She'd heard of pregnancy doing weird things to people, but this time Jules had gone completely mad. And too far.

'Jules?' Kat called, as Jules walked away.

'What?' Her face had that defiant look that Kat remembered so well. It was usually when she'd said or done something wrong. 'If you think I'm going to apologise — '

'No. I don't think that. I just wanted to say that your Eddie was quite right. It is none of your damn business.'

Jules looked as if she was about to say something more but before she could do so, the sound of applause made them both whirl round. It was Gerald Crabshaw, looking like he'd just got the ringside seat at the fight of the century and was determined to enjoy every moment of it. 'You go, girl,' he said. 'That told her.'

'I'm late for work,' Jules said and stomped away.

'No lunchtime shift for you, then, Katie?' he grinned.

She flushed. 'You know full well Donald fired me on Friday, seeing as you were the one instrumental in it.'

'Me?' He made a very poor fist at looking innocent. 'Oh no, you've got that all wrong. That was nothing to do with me.'

'Yeah, right. Of course it wasn't.'

'But as it happens, Donald was quite right,' he went on, his little piggy eyes gleaming. 'You're not exactly barmaid material, are you? Don't have the build for it for one thing. Way too skinny. Whereas young Julie there — ' His hands made a curvy arc that left Kat in no doubt what he was thinking about.

The creep. Without stopping to consider the wisdom of what she was saying, Kat lashed out. 'You know, Councillor Crabshaw, you never did say where you were the afternoon Marjorie was killed.'

She had the satisfaction of seeing that leery smirk wiped off his face. 'To quote what you said to your friend just now, it's none of your damn business,' he said icily.

'You know the police have let John Fleming go, don't you?' she pressed on recklessly. 'Apparently, he didn't do it. Makes you wonder who did, doesn't it?'

She had heard the expression of how the blood drains from a person's face but until that moment, she'd thought it was just another cliché, a writer's shortcut to rack up the tension. But she felt a moment of anxiety as Gerald's face went from an angry mottled red to chalky grey.

'I — I don't — ' he stammered, his eyes wide and scared. 'It — it wasn't — '

But, with the worst timing in the world, Kat's phone rang. She looked down, about to turn it off. But as she did so, Gerald Crabshaw turned tail and headed for the pub as if a hundred hellhounds were snapping at his heels.

11

Talk about saved by the bell. For a moment, it looked as if Gerald Crabshaw was going to say something incriminating before the ringing phone gave him the chance to gather his scattered wits and scuttle away. But her disappointment was mitigated when she saw the caller was Sean.

'Hi there, Kat Latcham,' he said, his voice as soft and beguiling as ever. 'I was wondering if you could meet me in Dintscombe? I've been thinking about what we were talking about last night. About a job. Are you still interested?'

Play it cool, Kat, she reminded herself. Don't let him know you're dying to bite his hand off. 'I may well be,' she said, in what she hoped was her coolest voice. 'You said about meeting up. When?'

'Like now, if you can make it. Do you have wheels?'

'Not any more.' Once again, she cursed

Ratface. She'd forgiven him for making off with her flatmate. But she'd never forgive him for making off with her car. 'I could maybe borrow Mum's. What sort of job?'

'Nothing official, I'm afraid, although who knows where it may lead? The thing is, I need someone in the field to do some — well, let's call it background research.'

'If it's background research you want, I'm your woman. When I worked for the radio station, I did most of the research for their flagship morning programme.'

She crossed her fingers tightly behind her back as she spoke. It was only a little white lie. He didn't need to know that most of the research she did consisted of trying to persuade the station's vanishing advertisers to come back. And she did once do a whole piece on threats to axe the local bus routes that Brad said was 'sparky and showed promise'.

'Yes, well, if it all works out, I'll make sure the editor knows about your contribution,' Sean said. 'Maybe we'll even get to share the byline. So you'll do it?'

'Provided it's legal,' she said.

'Of course it's legal. Trust me, I'm a journalist. Now, do you know the town park?'

'I should do,' she laughed. 'I had my first — and last — cigarette in the bandstand there when I was at school. I was sick for a week.'

'Well now, if I promise not to ply you with tobacco, would you meet me in the lay-by opposite the entrance and I'll explain? Are you up for it?'

Was she ever! Ten minutes later, after promising to treat her mother's sugar pink car as if it was made of spun glass, Kat was on her way to Dintscombe to meet Sean.

*   *   *

Dintscombe was not the liveliest place at the best of times. In one of the most short-sighted blunders Dintscombe District Council had ever made, they'd allowed an out of town retail park to open on the edge of the town eighteen months earlier and had then been surprised when it had

126

lured what few shoppers there had been away from the High Street and into their characterless, cloned retail units.

But Sundays in Dintscombe were about as bad as times could get. Kat half expected to see tumbleweed bowling towards her as she drove along the deserted High Street with its boarded-up shops, where a few scruffy pigeons scavenged among the overturned rubbish bins. She turned into the lay-by near the park where Sean was waiting for her.

He frowned as he opened the passenger door and got into the car, almost folding himself in two with the effort of shoehorning his long legs into Cheryl's little car, which seemed to have shrunk alarmingly. At the same time, Kat became acutely conscious of the musky tang of his aftershave and wished she'd taken more trouble over getting ready. Wished, too, she'd worn her skimpy blue top, instead of simply grabbing the first clean tee-shirt she came to.

'This is your car?' he asked.

'No. It's Mum's,' Kat said. 'She's the Cheryl — '

'Of Chez Cheryl. Yes, I kind of got that, seeing as it's emblazoned all over it.'

'She has this idea that if she drives around in an eye-catching car, people will see it and think, 'Oh yes, I must go and get my hair done. Chez Cheryl sounds a fun place.''

He raised an eyebrow. 'And do they?'

'Not so you'd notice. Although, as Dad says, at least it stops the boy racers pinching it.'

'He's not wrong there. The only thing is, Kat, I'm not sure it's quite suitable for the job I had in mind for you.'

Not suitable? Her excitement vanished, like a burst bubble. What had the car got to do with anything? 'Don't tell me.' She forced a laugh and was pleased at how casual her voice sounded. 'You're a boy racer at heart and wouldn't be seen dead in a sugar pink car?'

He grinned. 'Something like that. But what's more to the point is that it is a very conspicuous car, which might make it a very effective marketing tool for a hair salon, but probably not too well suited for a surveillance job.'

Kat's heart skipped a beat. 'Surveillance? As in private detectives? Stake outs and that sort of thing? Is that the research job you were talking about?' It certainly sounded a lot more interesting than colour coding the towels in her mum's airing cupboard. All she had to do was convince him that she and the car were up to the job. 'But I'll be very careful, I promise. Keep in the shadows. I'm sure it won't be a problem.'

He glanced at his watch and frowned. 'Well, it looks like we have no choice. I'm running out of time. Do you see that house over there?' He pointed to a small stone cottage with diamond paned windows and a neat pocket handkerchief front garden next to the park entrance. 'It belongs to a woman called Doreen Spetchley. Do you know her?'

'I don't think so. Should I?'

'Probably not. She works in the council planning office and I received a tip-off about her on Friday. A disgruntled work colleague whom she'd passed over for promotion said it might be worth my while checking who she's planning to meet this afternoon. But my informant wouldn't or couldn't say where that meeting would be. Or with whom.'

'So what do you want me to do? Wait and see who comes calling?'

'Exactly. Hence my concern about the car.'

'I'm sorry. Dad was using his so it was the Pink Peril or nothing. But I'll be really careful and stay in the shadows. What are you going to do?'

'That's why I called you. There's a massive fire on the industrial estate and the photographer's going to pick me up from here any minute. Could be a big story so I can't afford not to be there. So, how about it? Not your usual research job, I admit. But a pretty important one. Are you up for it?'

'Try and stop me.'

'Do you have a camera?'

'Only on this.' She showed him her phone.

'That'll probably be good enough. I don't want you to follow her or anything like that. Face it, that would be almost impossible driving around in a car like a big pink marshmallow. She'd spot you a mile off.'

'I'm sorry.'

'Don't be. It's probably a dead-end story anyway. If she goes out, chances are it will be to a car boot sale or something. But if the meeting is at her house and you can manage to get a shot of whoever it is going in, that would be amazing. And if you can get them both in the shot, so much the better. If not, well, at least we tried.'

Kat felt a warm glow at the way he said 'we tried'. Like they were a team. 'How will I know it's her?'

'She lives alone. She's in her mid-forties, slim, about five foot six with grey hair pulled back in one of those bun things or whatever you call them.'

'OK. I'll do what I can,' she said. 'I'll call you and — '

'Sorry. Got to go. This looks like my lift. I really appreciate this. I owe you one, Kat, so I do.'

As he and the photographer drove away, she settled down to watch out for Doreen Spetchley. It wasn't quite what she'd expected when Sean had talked about a research job. But a job was a job and who knew where this one would lead?

The only problem was, sitting with nothing to do but watch the little cottage for signs of life, gave her plenty of opportunity to do the one thing she hadn't wanted to do that afternoon which was to think about what Jules had said. She'd got it all wrong, of course. All that stuff about running home to mummy and walking into a job that was meant for someone else.

But most of all, Jules had been wrong about Will. Kat and Will were like brother and sister. They used to talk to each other about everything, even each others' romances — or, as was more often the case, lack of romances. Even when she left home and went to college, when she came back in the holidays, they'd take up where they'd left off. The best of mates. Until she met Ratface Nick. And everything changed. For a start, she didn't come home anything like so often and, when she did, Will was cold and distant, if not downright rude. And it had hurt.

As for this thing Jules had said about him 'fancying her', that was the most ridiculous thing she'd heard since the vicar's wife suggested a mass abseil down the church tower to raise money for the bell fund. In fact, not only was the thought of her and Will ridiculous, it was downright uncomfortable. They were like brother and sister, for pity's sake. It would be like fancying your own brother. Besides, how can you fancy a man who you could beat at conkers? Or who sat behind you in primary school and tied your plait to the back of a chair?

Suddenly she wished he was here beside her, so they could have a good laugh about how Jules's raging hormones had turned her brain to porridge. She'd be seeing little green men on the village pond next.

As if on cue, her phone pinged with a text message. From Jules. And, as expected, an apology. Of sorts. '*Sorry. Was a total cow this morning. Bad day. Weird things in pub lunchtime. CU later? xx*'

There was still no signs of activity from Doreen's cottage and Kat was getting bored — to say nothing of a numb bottom from sitting in the same place for too long. She replied to Jules, saying she'd call her tomorrow and then she texted Will. It was her turn to apologise. '*Srry abt last night. Not what u thought. Sean offered me work 4 Chronicle. Cldnt say no, cld I?!! Call u ltr. How's yr dad? Kat xxx*'

He probably wouldn't answer. But at least she'd tried. She'd just hit send when she saw the front door of the cottage open. It was Doreen Spetchley. It had to be. Sean's description was spot on. Kat watched with dismay as she hurried out and got into the small blue hatchback that was parked on the drive.

Obviously the meeting was not at Doreen's house. What to do now? Sean had told her not to attempt to follow her, but she couldn't just sit here and do nothing. Surely, as long as she kept a couple of cars between her and Doreen, it would be easy enough? Goodness knows, she'd watched enough detective programmes on the television.

★ ★ ★

Kat's hands were shaking as she switched on the engine and waited for Doreen to drive past. She waited for another car to pass before pulling out, earning herself a blast on the horn from the irate four by four driver she'd just cut in front of.

According to the wags in the Mucky Duck, since the latest round of cutbacks to rural policing it was easier to find a Lesser Spotted Furblewitt in Dintscombe and the surrounding villages than a policeman. Which was fortunate for Kat, because if a policeman had been around that Sunday afternoon, he'd have breath-alysed her for erratic driving quicker than you could say 'Could you blow into the bag, please?'

One moment, she was crawling at a snail's pace in an effort to keep at least one car between her and Doreen, the next she'd be racing along, the engine of her mum's little pink car screaming as she rushed to catch up. They made tailing someone look so easy on the television, but the reality was a nightmare.

At one time, she got stuck behind a bus and for one scary moment thought she'd lost Doreen completely, and only by a piece of good luck was able to nip past the bus in time to see Doreen indicating left.

As they left the town on the bypass, Kat was able to relax a little and allow a few more cars between them. But her relaxed mood didn't last as she then began to worry about what she would do if Doreen was heading for Millford Magna. It would be almost impossible to follow her along the narrow lanes that led into the village without being noticed. She gave a sigh of relief when she saw the blue hatchback indicating one turning before the one for the village.

Suddenly, Kat had a pretty good idea where Doreen might be making for. The narrow road led up to Compton Woods, used only by a few local dog walkers and bird watchers. It was the perfect spot for a secret assignation.

Kat pulled in at the bottom of the hill that wound up through a tunnel of trees to the car park near the top. The last thing she wanted to do was catch up with Doreen part way up the hill. Suddenly she got a mirror full of headlights and pulled over as close to the hedge as she dared to let a silver Porsche rocket by.

She turned her head away quickly as she recognised the driver. It was Gerald Chapman. What on earth was he doing up here on a Sunday afternoon? She didn't have him down as a bird watcher and he was well known for his dislike of dogs.

She waited until Gerald's Porsche was out of sight then began very slowly to drive up the hill. She knew this area well as she and Will used to come up here collecting hazel nuts when they were children and she remembered that just before the entrance to the car park was a field gate. She drove as quietly as she could, parked in the gateway and got out, being careful not to slam the door as she did so.

Then she crept up the remaining few yards to the car park and, hidden by the screen of hazel bushes, peered in. There were just two cars in there. Doreen's little blue hatchback and Gerald's sleek silver Porsche.

The two of them were standing, very close together, Doreen's long thin arms draped around his neck. Doreen Spetchley and Gerald Crabshaw, having an affair. More to the point, someone who worked in the Planning Department wrapped around a member of the Council's Planning Committee, tangled together like tights in a washing machine. What a story. Sean was going to be delighted.

Kat felt in her pocket for her phone and groaned. Of all the stupid things. She'd only left the wretched thing in the car.

She was about to turn away to go back and fetch it when there was a sudden dramatic change in the body language between the two. Doreen pulled away, her hands to her mouth, obviously in some distress. Gerald looked uncomfortable but made no move towards her. In fact, he stepped back as Doreen reached both hands towards him, as if she was imploring him. He shook his head and began to move towards his car.

Kat stepped back in alarm. If Gerald turned left out of the car park and went back down the hill, he couldn't fail to see her mother's pink car in the gateway.

She'd already upset him once today. And she wasn't too keen on doing so again. She hurried back towards her car, but hadn't got very far before she heard the sound of a car coming down the hill towards her.

12

She ran for the car and had just jumped in when Doreen's blue hatchback hurtled past. Kat caught a brief glimpse of her contorted face, but whether it was from rage or grief, it was impossible to tell.

So where was Gerald? She heard the throaty roar of a powerful engine bursting into life. She pressed the button that activated the central locking and wriggled down in the seat as far out of sight as it was possible to go in the small car. With a bit of luck, Gerald, like Doreen, would be so wound up he'd drive past without seeing her.

The sound of the car carrying on up the hill, rather than coming back down towards her, left her weak with relief and she started breathing again. Time, she reckoned, to turn the car around and make a hasty exit. She couldn't risk going up to the car park, just in case the car she'd heard had not been Gerald's and he was still there. There was nothing for it but to do a three point turn in the narrow road where there was little room for manoeuvre.

It wasn't exactly a three point turn. In fact, she lost count of how many shuffles it took. Certainly, it would have made a driving test examiner reach for his failure notice, particularly as on the final shuffle, she went back too far too quickly and there was an ominous crunch as the car connected with the heavy metal gate.

That car was top of her mother's Best Loved List, ahead of the cat, George Clooney and her dad. Kat would have dropped off the list completely and was going to be sweeping the salon and unwinding perm rollers for the rest of her life when her mother saw what she'd done to her precious car.

As she reached the bypass, Kat took the road back to Dintscombe again. She told herself that she was concerned about Doreen and wanted to check that she'd got back safely. But the truth was, she was not in any great hurry to face her mother. When she drove past Doreen's cottage the little blue hatchback was parked on the drive. She pulled in to the lay-by and called Sean.

'Any news?' he asked.

'You'd better believe it,' she said. 'She was only meeting our esteemed Councillor Crabshaw.'

'I knew it,' he breathed. 'I knew there was something dodgy about that fellow. I'll bet you what you like she's been passing on confidential stuff to him. It has to be something like that. Remember that new retail development?'

'You mean the one that was supposed to be out of town that turned out to be close enough to the town centre to kill the High Street?'

'That's the one. The Planning Committee were seriously misled about the original application and I'm pretty sure your Councillor Crabshaw had something to do with that. If he was in cahoots with someone in the Planning Department, that makes it seem even more likely.'

'They're having an affair, that's for sure,' she said. 'Or, put it this way, they looked as if things between them were pretty hot, judging by the way they were tangled up together.'

'On her front doorstep?' Sean sounded surprised. 'I wouldn't have thought Gerald Crabshaw would have been that indiscreet.'

'He wasn't. I — I know you said not to but I followed her.'

'You followed her?' Sean sounded annoyed. 'Damn right I told you not to. That was a pretty stupid thing to do.'

'She didn't see me, honest,' Kat said quickly. 'They met in the car park up in Compton Woods. I know the area well from when I used to play up there as a kid, so I parked in a gateway and went up through the bushes. I used to be very good at tracking, you know.'

'Did you now?' He laughed softly. 'Well, you showed initiative, that's for sure. Even so, you might have been putting yourself in danger. I would hate to lose my bright new research assistant when I've only just found her. Promise me next time, you'll do what I say.'

Next time? There was going to be a next time? She glowed in the warmth of his praise. Suddenly, the worry about what she was going to say to her mother faded into insignificance. 'That's when I saw them, cuddled up together. But he must have said something to upset her because they suddenly broke apart and stalked back to their respective cars. Talk about hell hath no fury. She looked spitting mad fit to burst as she drove off. I was actually a bit worried about her, which is why I came back here to her cottage, just to check she got home in one piece. Which she did.'

'You've done a brilliant job.' She glowed some more until he added: 'Did you manage to get any pictures?'

'No. I'm sorry.' Now this was the tricky bit. Should she confess that she'd left her phone in the car or try and brazen it out? She decided to go for a half truth. 'It was really difficult. I couldn't get too close in case they saw me.'

'Not to worry. You've given me something to work on now. I'm grateful to you.'

'How's your fire going?'

'Pretty good. They're being a bit tight-lipped at the moment, but it looks as if they suspect arson. They say they'll have a statement any moment now. So, once again, I'm just hanging around waiting.'

'I'd happily swap with you,' she said wistfully. 'I've got to go home and face my mother.'

'Ah now, you're not telling me you've gone and dinged the pink marshmallow, are you?'

'I'm afraid so. I had to do rather a hasty three point turn and, well, let's just say, there was an incident between the car and a metal gate and the car came off worse.'

'That's tough. And I'm sorry I can't put that down on my expenses for you, otherwise I would. However, I do have a mate who's very good at knocking out dents. He'll do you a good job and not rip you off.'

'I'll bear it in mind, thanks. I've got a feeling I'm going to be paying for my error of judgement in unpaid labour in the salon until the end of the century.'

★　★　★

She took her time driving back to the village and, once there, turned up the hill towards the farm instead of going home. She thought she'd call in and see if Will was about. He wasn't. But his father was.

It was difficult to decide whether John Fleming looked better or worse than the last time she'd seen him. Then, he'd been white-faced, unshaven and shocked as he was driven away in the back of a police car. Now, he was still white-faced, but clean-shaven, his hair smoothed tidily back and his clothes, though crumpled, looked clean.

But his eyes were as empty and haunted as ever.

'It's good to see you home again, Mr Fleming,' Kat said. 'How are you?'

'How am I?' He frowned as if he was having to dig deep to find the answer to that question. 'I'm sober. That's what I am. But where are my manners? Come along in, Katie, please do. Will is off on the farm somewhere but he'll be back shortly.'

She followed him down the long gloomy passage and into the kitchen, which was marginally tidier than the last time she'd seen it. He stood on one side of the large deal table, she stood on the other.

Kat swallowed. This was awkward. What did she say now? 'I — I hope you're feeling better.'

He shook his head. 'Anything but, lass,' he sighed. 'Anything but. At least the drinking stopped me thinking and feeling. But now, I don't know. I just don't know.'

Her heart contracted with pity for him. He looked lost and broken. 'Have you seen a doctor?'

'Of course not. What would he do? Tell me to give up drinking, that's what.' The knuckles on his hands showed white where he gripped the back of a chair so tightly. 'The police still think I killed her, you know.'

'Then they're wrong. Because you didn't,' Kat said fiercely.

'No. No. You're quite right, I didn't. And Will tells me how you've gone around defending me to everyone, for which I'm grateful. But, you know, when they put me in that police cell and shut

147

the door, I thought — for a moment then, I thought maybe I had.' Kat had to strain to hear him as his voice dropped to a faint whisper. 'And that was what scared me. It also made me see what a monster I'd become. That I could have killed someone and not even remembered it. I thought, too, how ashamed and disgusted Sally would be. That was what Marjorie said to me that day and she was absolutely right. Which was why I was so furious with her. Because I knew she spoke nothing but the truth.'

'But you didn't kill her.'

'No. I didn't kill her. But I came damn close to killing myself with my stupid drinking. Goodness knows what would have happened to me if the Farm Shop hadn't been locked that afternoon.'

'How do you mean?'

'After I'd had the run in with Marjorie, I stormed into the house, grabbed the whisky bottle and went up to my room. But there was only a bit left in that bottle, so I went out across the yard to the shop, where I used to keep a stash. But I figured Will must have found it — he'd found all the ones in the house — and locked the door to keep me out. Goodness knows what state I'd have been in if I'd found those bottles. As it was, I drank enough to blot out the whole of the rest of that day.'

'You don't remember going in the bar that night? I was working there. I served you.'

He shook his head. 'I don't remember a thing until I came round next morning with you and Will standing over me and Will asking me what the hell I'd done.'

'Wait a minute,' Kat said. 'Go back a bit. You said Will must have found your stash. Where did you say you kept it?'

'In the Farm Shop. Down behind one of the freezers.'

'But Will hasn't set foot in the place since his mother died. He told me he couldn't face it and last week, when we found poor Marjorie, was the first time.'

'He couldn't face going in the shop?' John looked troubled. 'Poor lad. I — I didn't know. He always seemed so together, I thought he was ok. I didn't know.'

Kat sighed. 'Don't you two ever talk to each other? About things other than the farm, I mean? No, I don't suppose you do. It's not your way, is it?'

John shook his head. 'I didn't know,' he repeated the words as if it was some kind of mantra.

'But, if it wasn't Will who locked the door, then who?' Kat asked, her eyes suddenly wide as she realised the implication of what she was saying.

John caught on at the same time. His face went even whiter, his eyes even more shocked. 'You mean, the murderer was in there? At that very moment when I tried the door? That he — ?' He put his face in his hands. 'Oh, dear God, what have I done? What have I done?'

'Come and sit down,' Kat said gently as she led him towards a chair. 'You look as if you're about to keel over. And John, you haven't done anything.'

It was the first time in her life she'd ever called him anything other than Mr Fleming, but the use of his christian name came naturally, her only thought was concern for him.

'Can I get you anything?' she asked. 'Tea? Brandy?'

He shook his head violently. 'I swear, Katie, I will never touch alcohol again for as long as I live. As for you saying I didn't do anything, you don't get it, do you? Because that's just the point. If I hadn't been so stinking drunk, I would have gone back to the house and found my key. I might have saved Marjorie's life.'

Kat stared at him helplessly, not knowing what to say or do.

'See?' He looked at her intently. 'You think so too.'

'No, of course I don't. You can't torture yourself like that,' she said, desperate to get through to him. 'We can all blame ourselves for one thing or another. If I'd listened to her more carefully that morning, I'd have maybe been able to tell the police who it was she was going to have it out with. Who had got her dander up, as she put it.'

'She was talking about me.'

'No she wasn't. I'm absolutely certain about that because she'd already had a go about you.' Kat felt her cheeks redden.

'Jeez, I'm sorry. I — I didn't mean — '

'It's ok.' He gave a wry smile. 'I think I can guess exactly what she was saying about me. I'll say this for Marjorie, she would never say anything behind your back that she wasn't prepared to say to your face.'

'That's true. So, who was she planning to meet after she left you? Did she say?'

He shook his head. 'Not that I can recall, I'm afraid. But to be honest, she could have said she was off to have tea with Elvis and it wouldn't have registered, I was that hopping mad with her.'

'I don't think she approved of Elvis either,' Kat said, trying to lessen the tension, if only for a moment.

His brief smile didn't reach his eyes. 'I've made a terrible, terrible mess of things, haven't I?' he sighed. 'It wasn't until I saw Will, that day he came to collect me from the police station that I realised how selfish I've been and how much I've let fall on his shoulders. I vowed there and then that if I get out of this mess without going to prison, I'll work my socks off to make things right again between us. I can hardly look him in the face and that's the truth.'

'And have you told him that?' Kat said quietly.

'No. But I will.'

'Promise?'

'I promise.' He reached out and took her hand. 'Thank you for believing in me, Katie.'

Kat blinked back a tear. 'That's what friends are for,' she said gruffly.

'Yes. Yes.' John's eyes, Kat was glad to see, looked a little less bleak, as if talking had cleared some of the fog that was weighing him down. 'You're a good girl. Sally always said you were one of the best and she was a good judge of people was my Sally. I'm so glad you and Will have made it up.'

'You know what we're like,' Kat murmured. 'Fighting like cat and dog one minute, best mates the next.'

'Do you know, Sally always hoped that you and Will might make a go of it one day.'

'A go of it? What? You mean — ?' Kat floundered, her cheeks getting redder and hotter. 'There's nothing like that between us, you know. Nothing at all. We're just mates, that's all.'

'There's not? I'm sorry to hear it,' he said quietly. 'Sorry, too, if I embarrassed you. You see? It's not always good to talk, is it? There are some things that are better left unsaid.'

'Yeah, well, maybe you're right.' She stood up to go. Will could well be back any minute and she wanted to be out of the way before he did. Suddenly, facing her mother's anger about the car seemed the easier option.

★   ★   ★

As Kat passed the pub on her way home, she was surprised to see Gerald's car in the car park. She checked her watch. It was almost four o'clock. Way past Donald's normal closing time. And the pub door was shut. If she hadn't known otherwise, she'd have assumed Gerald had had a heavy lunchtime session and had decided to leave his car and walk home.

Was Donald having a lock-in? It would

be the first time ever. She stopped the car to get a closer look and, as she did so, the pub door opened and Gerald came out. He stopped dead when he saw her and, before Kat could realise his intentions, he hurried across and wrenched open the car door.

She gave a little scream as he thrust his angry face into the car.

'What the hell do you think you are doing?' he roared. 'Are you following me?'

'Of course I'm not. I'm on my way home.'

'It was you, wasn't it? You were up Compton Woods earlier. Don't try to deny it. I saw you.'

'I — I was trying to find my dog.'

'You don't have a dog.' His voice went up several decibels.

'I — No. Did I say my dog? I meant Elsie Flintlock's little dog. I — I've just taken him home. Elsie was ever so grateful. Well, I must be off. Mum will be wondering where I am.'

'Good idea. Oh, and Katie — ' Kat pressed against the window as he leaned in still further. 'Keep your sticky little beak out of things that don't concern you. OK?'

'OK,' she squeaked and her legs were shaking so much that the car went down the High Street in a series of hops that would have impressed a kangaroo.

13

Kat crawled out of bed next morning, feeling as if she hadn't slept a wink all night. Every time she drifted off, images of Marjorie, half in, half out of the freezer, became superimposed on various images of Gerald Crabshaw's angry face. Sometimes she saw him in the bar, ranting on about Marjorie. Other times it would be when he'd accosted her in the street yesterday and accused her of following him. But each time, his snarling message had been the same.

Keep your sticky little beak out of my business. Remember what happened to Marjorie.

Kat would then be jerked back to wakefulness, bathed in sweat, her heart banging against her rib cage like a trapped canary. Gerald was Marjorie's killer. She was sure of it. The thing was, what to do about it?

But, of course, in the clear light of day

her fears, which had seemed so real and frightening in the small hours, now seemed irrational and unfounded. The truth, she realised, was probably something much more mundane. Yes, Gerald was a nasty piece of work, a total sleaze bag, in fact. And, as Sean suspected, it was highly likely he was abusing his position as a member of the planning committee to get up to something iffy. It would probably also explain his fling with Doreen Spetchley. The rather plain, grey woman was not his usual type at all.

But like all bullies, he was nothing but bluster. She was willing to bet he was trying to cover up his affair with Doreen. Nothing more sinister than that. Marjorie's killer had to be a stranger. The poor soul had simply been in the wrong place at the wrong time.

Even so, she thought it would be a good thing to tell Sean about the threat Gerald had made. She'd tried his phone several times that morning, but each time she'd got his voice mail and she decided against leaving a message, apart from asking him to call her.

Ten minutes later, her phone rang. She snatched it up but was disappointed to see the caller was Jules, not Sean.

'Fancy coming round for coffee?' Jules asked. 'Well, coffee for you. I still can't face it.'

The truth was, Kat couldn't face another lecture from Jules this morning. She glanced around the empty salon. 'I'm not sure I can get away,' she said quietly. 'Mum would have me scrubbing the floor with a nail brush if she could find one.'

'That bad, eh?'

'Worse. The thing is, you see, I had a little prang in the car yesterday and she's making me work it off. Another time, eh?'

'For goodness sake go,' Cheryl said, coming in behind her. 'Get out from under my feet for a bit, or I really will have you scrubbing the floor with a nail brush. You're looking really peaky this morning. Go out and get some fresh air.'

'OK, Jules,' Kat said. 'It looks like I've just been given some time out for good behaviour. I'll come round, shall I? Unless you want to come here?'

'You come to me. I've got some

chocolate tea cakes I need to share, otherwise I'll end up as wide as I'm high by the time this baby is born.'

Kat laughed. 'You remember my weakness, then?'

'I remember all your weaknesses, girl,' she said. 'But I won't go on about them, I promise. I'm really sorry about yesterday. I was way out of order. Forgiven?'

Ten minutes later, Kat was moving a pair of fairy wings and a glittery plastic tiara from a chair in Jules's cramped, chaotic kitchen. She was on her second tea cake when Jules said: 'I meant what I said. I'm sorry for letting rip yesterday. You had every right to tell me to mind my own business. Eddie says living with me is like living on the edge of an active volcano, just waiting for the next eruption.'

'He said that?' Kat was impressed. Eddie must have paid more attention in geography lessons than she'd given him credit for. 'Does he know about the baby yet?'

Jules nodded. 'Actually, he was pretty cool about it. More cool than I am to be honest, but then, he's not the one being sick every single day.'

'Still bad, eh?'

'The tablets the doctor gave me last week are helping a bit but it's still not great. But hey, I didn't ask you round here so I could whinge on about morning sickness. I wanted to say I was sorry. To your face.'

'Which you've done, so let's forget it, eh?' Kat said, eager to change the subject. 'So, what did you mean in your text when you said something weird happened in the pub lunch time yesterday?'

'Did I?' Jules frowned. 'Oh yes. It was Gerald Crabshaw. I wanted to ask you what on earth you did to him to freak him out. He came in to the pub not long after I did in a right state. Ordered a double whisky and his hands were shaking that much I thought he was going to spill it. Then he knocked it back like he was dying of thirst. Yet, less than five minutes earlier, when he spoke to us — '

'Overheard us having a spat, more like it.'

'Whatever.' Jules flicked some chocolatey

crumbs from her blouse. 'But he was his usual pervy self, wasn't he? So what on earth did you say to him?'

'Me? Nothing much. Well, I had a go at him about getting me the sack and then asked him where he was the afternoon Marjorie was killed. That didn't go down too well, as you can imagine.'

Jules's eyes widened. 'Hey, if they hadn't arrested John Fleming, it would almost make you think he'd done it, wouldn't it?'

'John was released without charge yesterday. Gerald didn't look too pleased when I told him that, I can tell you.' Suddenly, all her doubts from her sleepless night came flooding back. 'He could have done it, you know.'

'You've got to be kidding,' Jules laughed. 'He's all mouth and trousers, that one. Say boo to him and he'd run a mile. Come on, Kat. This is Gerald Crabshaw we're talking about. We've known him all our lives. And whilst he's a right pain in the proverbial, particularly since he was elected councillor, he's no murderer.'

'No. Of course he isn't. You're right, of course.' Kat decided against telling her friend how she'd seen Gerald up in Compton Woods with Doreen. She didn't want to tell anyone. At least, not until she'd talked it through with Sean. Instead she said: 'It's just that I saw him again yesterday afternoon, about four o'clock. He'd just come out of the pub and he threatened me. Said if I didn't stop poking my nose into his business, I'd come to a very sticky end, or words to that effect. And the thing that spooked me was not only the look on his face as he said it but the fact that he'd said the same thing to me before, almost word for word, only then he'd been talking about Marjorie — the day before Will and I found her body.'

Jules chewed her fingernail. 'Even so, he was only mouthing off, surely? You know what he was like. He was always going on about Marjorie, ever since he got done for drunk driving and reckoned it was her who'd tipped the police off. Which, knowing Marjorie, it probably was.'

'Yeah. You're right, of course.' Her friend's common sense approach had just lifted a huge weight from Kat's shoulders. At one time in the night she'd actually convinced herself she should tell the police about Gerald's threat. But now, she could see, it was just an over-reaction on her part. And anyway, she might then have to explain to them what she'd been doing up in Compton Woods yesterday which could have been a tad tricky. 'I expect I'd just caught him on a bad day.'

'You're not kidding he was having a bad day. According to Elsie Flintlock, he'd had a bit of a go at Donald, as well,' Jules said.

'What about?'

'I don't know. I wasn't there. Donald had sent me out to the store room and when I came back Gerald had gone and Elsie said that he'd yelled at Donald and stormed out.'

'What about?'

'She didn't say. Here, for goodness sake have another of these.' She pushed the packet of tea cakes across the table. 'Otherwise I'll eat the lot.'

'I thought you said you couldn't
thing?' Kat said.

'Anything except chocolate tea c
Jules said.

Kat reached across for another tea
but before she could take one, her p
rang. It was Sean.

'Sorry,' she said to Jules. 'I've got to
this. Hi Sean. Thanks for ringing bac

'No problem. Sorry it took so long
things have been pretty hectic here
morning. What's up?'

She glanced across at Jules who
straining to hear every word, while a
same time pretending she wasn't. 'Ca
meet sometime today? So that I can
you . . . the, um, results of that resear
did for you yesterday.'

'Today could be tricky. Tomorr
better.'

'Tomorrow will be fine.'

'Then how about we — look, s
Kat, I've got to go. Mike's making fra
signals at me. Looks like something
may have come in. I'll call you.'

'Great. See you then. Bye.'

Jules was grinning at her. 'Resea

h? Is that what they call it now?'

'That was a guy from the Chronicle,' Kat said. 'It's purely business.'

'Now, would this be the dishy Irishman who was asking after you in the pub on Saturday?'

'You think he's dishy? I can't say I'd noticed,' Kat said in what she hoped was a casual voice.

'Hah, not much you hadn't. I can tell the way your cheeks have turned the colour of beetroot. You never could keep a secret from me, Katie Latcham. It was him, wasn't it?'

'Yes, and Dad gave him my mobile number, can you believe it? He could have been an axe murderer for all Dad knew.'

'What did he want you for?' Jules asked.

'My body. What else?' Kat laughed.

'Yeah, well. That goes without saying. You know he's got a bit of a reputation, don't you?'

'For what?' Kat knew she shouldn't ask but couldn't help herself.

'For loving and leaving them. You remember Ginny Mason in the year below us at school? Curly hair and freckles. Had a thing about Johnny Depp. She went out with him for a while, things were really serious between them until he dropped her like a stone for no apparent reason. Then there was the girl who works in Dintscombe Library and after that — '

'OK. OK. I get the picture,' Kat said, more rattled than she wanted to let on. 'There's nothing between me and Sean. Nor likely to be. Yes, I did meet him Saturday night, but it was strictly business. As a matter of fact, he offered me a job.'

'On the Chronicle?' Jules looked impressed. 'Doing what?'

'Well, it's just helping out with the odd bit of background research at the moment which is what I wanted to talk to him about. But who knows where it might lead?'

'With Sean Ryan, I think I can probably guess,' Jules said, her face suddenly serious. 'You will be careful, Kat, won't you?'

'What, like you're my mother all of a sudden?' Kat snapped.

'No. But I am your friend. And I wouldn't want you to get hurt. You know he's going around asking all sorts of questions about the murder, don't you?'

'Well, of course he is,' Kat said. 'He's a journalist. Asking questions is what he does.'

'That and making up the answers if he doesn't get the right ones,' Jules said.

'Well, don't you worry about me. I can take care of myself,' Kat said as she stood up to go.

'Oh no. Now I've upset you again. Me and my big mouth. Oh, for pity's sake, don't go off in a strop again.'

'I'm not in a strop, honest,' Kat said. 'But I really do have to go. Mum will have steam coming out of her ears if I'm not back soon.'

'So how did you come to prang her car?'

Kat grimaced. 'I reversed into a gate.' Again, Kat decided not to tell her where the gate was or what was doing when she reversed into it. 'But you know how Mum is about that wretched car. I'll never be able to borrow it again and will have to spend the rest of my life apologising to her. Thanks for the coffee and tea cakes.

I'll see you soon, ok?'

'Yeah, let's do that,' Jules said as she opened the front door to see Kat out. As she did so, they saw Will coming down the road towards them.

'What I said yesterday, about Will having a thing for you,' Jules said quickly, putting a hand on Kat's arm. 'I wouldn't want you to get the wrong impression. That Will's some sad loser, pining away for you.'

'No, of course I didn't think that.' Kat forced a laugh. 'You forget, Jules, I know Will a lot better than you do.'

Jules took her hand away and waved at Will. She lowered her voice and went on: 'In fact, according to Eddie, he's seeing this vet who works in the practice in Dintscombe. Name of Anneka, or something like that. She's Swedish, he says.'

'That's great. I'm pleased for him.'

Of course she was pleased for him. But why, then, did she have this weird feeling, the sort you get when you put your foot on a step that isn't there?

It was her disturbed night catching up on her. That was all.

14

'Hi Will,' Jules called out to him. 'What are you doing hanging around here on a Monday morning? Have you been given time off for good behaviour as well?'

'Something like that,' he grinned.

'Got time for a coffee?'

'Sorry, I can't stop. I came to find Katie. Her mum said she was down here.'

Kat shot him a worried glance. 'You were looking for me?' she asked. It would have to be something pretty heavy to drag him away from the farm on a week day morning. 'What for?' Her heart missed a beat. 'It's not your dad, is it?'

'No. He's fine.' He looked across at Jules then back to Kat. She'd always been able to read the expressions on his face. This one was saying that whatever he had to say to her, he'd prefer not to do so in front of Jules. She nodded to show she'd got the message.

'Are you on your way back?' he went

on. 'Only if you are, I'll walk with you.'

'And I've got a million things to do,' Jules said as she turned to go back indoors. 'See you both.'

As they walked off, Kat saw a curtain twitch in the house and grinned. Jules might well have a million things to do but watching them was obviously right up there at the top of that list.

'So come on, out with it. What was so important that you had to come and seek me out, rather than phone?' she asked once they were safely out of earshot. 'You haven't lost your phone again, have you? Honestly, Will, you're the limit.'

'No, I haven't.'

'Then where is it? No, don't tell me. On the dresser in your kitchen.'

'Something like that. If you must know I was coming down to see your mum anyway. I had a nice leg of lamb I thought she might like. I know how your dad enjoys his roast lamb and after what happened the last time I went to find a piece of meat for your mum — '

'Oh no, please, Will. Don't remind me. As you say,' she went on quickly before the flashback to that moment could take hold, 'Dad is certainly very partial to roast lamb. And if it gets Mum off her current diet and back to real food, you'll have done us all a favour. So, does that mean the police have let you back in the farm shop then?'

'No. It's still taped off. They were rooting around in there again this morning. From the little bit they let slip, it doesn't look like they've found the murder weapon yet. They've now been able to rule out Dad's shotgun, which is a huge relief.'

'I can imagine. And your dad is ok, isn't he? I mean, you weren't just saying that because Jules was there?'

'No, honest. He's a lot better. He's still very shaken by it all, of course. Well, we both are.'

'Yes, I know how you feel.'

Kat never used to have a problem over what to say to Will. In fact, he used to complain that she never stopped talking. But for the moment, she couldn't think of anything to say. Well, not strictly true. She had plenty to say. Her problem was, where to start? They walked on in awkward silence for a while. Then they both spoke at once.

'Look, I'm sorry about — ' she said.

'You see the thing is — ' he said and gestured her to carry on.

'I just wanted to explain about Saturday night. In the pub. With Sean.'

'Sean?' His eyes darkened.

'Sean Ryan. He's — '

'A reporter on the Chronicle,' his eyes darkened even further, his face creased into a scowl. 'I know who he is. He's been plaguing the life out of me and Dad, asking us for an interview.'

'OK. But I just wanted to tell you that the meeting I had with him in the Queen's Arms on Saturday night was business, not pleasure, ok?'

'Really?' One eyebrow shot up. 'From where I was standing, it looked like a whole heap of pleasure.'

'And if you'd looked a little more carefully, you'd have seen that I was drinking mineral water and had a file full of my work with me. Hardly the stuff of a hot date, is it?' She glared at him.

'Besides, what were you doing there? You always said you hated that hippy drippy folksy music.'

He grinned at her as they crossed the road in to the village's main street. 'I do. But they serve a good pint in there.'

'Yes, that's what Sean said.' And, of course, the niggly little voice inside her head went on, Anneka or whatever her name was, probably liked hippy, drippy folksy music. So where had she been Saturday night? Was that why he had been in such a bad mood?

They walked on in awkward silence for a few minutes. 'Well, I'm glad your dad's ok,' she said eventually. 'I was worried about him.'

Will stopped and turned to face her. 'As a matter of fact, that's what I wanted to talk to you about. Well, not about him, as such. But what you and Dad were talking about yesterday.' He looked down at his hands. 'He — he told me, you know.'

Kat's face burned. So John had told Will that Sally had always hoped he and Kat would 'make a go of it', as he'd put it,

174

had he? Great. Absolutely great. How was she going to get out of this one?

'Oh, well, that's parents for you, isn't it?' she mumbled, scuffing the edge of the pavement with the toe of her boot. 'Always making plans.'

'Plans about what?' He stared at her blankly. 'Sorry. You've lost me.'

'It doesn't matter,' she said quickly. 'I was just wittering. Forget it. What were you saying?'

'Dad said you'd told him how I hadn't been able to face going in the shop since — since Mum died.' He plucked at the fastening of his coat with restless fingers. 'He — he also said you'd told him that he and I should talk. About how we felt about losing Mum. And all that.'

'And did you?' she asked gently.

He nodded. 'Sort of. He said he thought I blamed him for being so wrapped up in the farm that he hadn't noticed Mum's illness. Can you believe that? As if I would.'

'Maybe he blames himself?'

'That's just as daft. And I told him so. He then said he'd no idea about the strain I'd been under and that he felt really bad about it. Promised to make it up to me. He's sober, you know. Hasn't touched a drop since he was arrested.'

'I know. He told me.'

He placed his hands on her shoulders, his expression serious. 'You're a star, Katie Latcham, that's what you are.'

'I didn't do anything — '

'You believed in him when no one else did. And you cared enough to talk some sense into him. Into both of us. And for that we're both really grateful. Thanks to you, we've cleared the air a bit. Dad and I are both as bad as each other when it comes to talking about how we feel about things. And people.'

Kat opened her mouth to make some light hearted remark in an effort to break the tension that had sprung up between them, but nothing came out. Instead, she stood as if frozen, staring at him, and wondering why she'd never noticed before how in this light his eyes were the colour of cornflowers and how he had a little fan of white lines in the corner of each eye, made no doubt from screwing up his eyes against the sunlight.

'Th-that's blokes for you,' she finally managed to say in a voice that didn't sound remotely like her own.

'Yes, well.' He cleared his throat and raked his fingers through his hair. 'So this morning, good as his word, Dad said he'd handle things on the farm today and that I was to take you somewhere for lunch. As a thank you. From us both.'

'Oh, there's no need,' she said quickly, relieved that the moment of weirdness between them, whatever it was, had passed. 'I only did what any mate would have done. Besides, I'm just on my way to see Elsie Flintlock.'

'I'm sorry but my lunch invitation doesn't include her,' he said.

Kat laughed. 'Thank goodness for that. It's just that she — she's got something for me. Something I need for this research work I'm doing for the Chronicle. The one I was talking to Sean about on Saturday night. You know, memories and all that.'

It wasn't exactly a lie, but she was uncomfortably aware that it wasn't exactly the whole truth either and was relieved when he didn't follow it up.

'It's always wise to put a time limit on a visit to Elsie, otherwise you'll be there all day.' He looked at his watch. 'How about I pick you up about twelve and we'll take a run down to the coast? I thought we could go and see if that cafe on the beach still does those amazing crab sandwiches. I haven't been there for years.'

She scrabbled around frantically for a convincing sounding excuse. For a reason she couldn't even explain to herself, she didn't want to go out to lunch with him. Was it because of John telling her how he and Sally had hoped that she and Will might have made a go of it, as he'd put it? Or Jules telling her about Will and the sexy Swedish vet? Or Will, asking her out, not because he wanted to, but because his dad told him to?

'Oh, Will, I'd love to, but the problem is Mum. I'm working for her all this week. Well, the rest of my life probably. I suppose you know what I did to her car? I should imagine she's told the whole world by now.'

'I saw the damage. You must have given

something a hefty clunk. What was it?'

'A metal gate. I was trying to do a three point turn and got it wrong.' She decided not to tell him the metal gate had been up near Compton Woods, nor what she was doing there. That information was on a strictly need to know basis and she decided that Will, like Jules, didn't need to know. 'So, I don't think Mum would be too happy if I skived off.'

'Your mum said she's fed up with you moping about the place and grumbling at everything from her choice of music to the colour of the curtains — '

'I didn't grumble about the curtains. I just suggested, very tactfully, that the salon needed a bit of a makeover, that's all. As for the music, how would you like to spend all morning listening to Des O'Connor? She says the customers like him. But honestly . . . '

'Anyway, she said she's tired of you mooching about the place and would be much obliged to me for taking you out from under her feet,' he said. 'So, are you up for it? Or have you got something more exciting planned? More business meetings with smooth-talking Irish journos, maybe? You haven't told me anything about this job he's talking about. What exactly is it?'

Time, Kat decided, for a quick change of subject. She had also run out of excuses. 'Twelve o'clock will be fine,' she said as she waited for a small minibus to drive past before she crossed the road. 'Can you pick me up from Mum's?'

'Better had. I'd hate to start Elsie Flintlock's tongue wagging again.'

'Hah! I don't think that would be possible. That would be to assume it ever stopped wagging in the first place.'

* * *

Elsie opened the front door and screamed, 'Come back here NOW.'

Kat flattened herself against the wall as something small, fast and hairy hurtled towards her, shot through her legs and disappeared out of the front gate.

'Would you like me to go and get him back?' Kat asked.

'No point. The little monster will be

180

half-way to Dintscombe by now. He'll come back when he's hungry.'

Elsie's little dog, whose brown and white fur always reminded Kat of a worn-down toothbrush, was of dubious parentage and even more dubious temperament. His name was Prescott and he was notorious for biting first and asking questions later.

'Did you want something?' Elsie asked. 'Or are you one of those detractor burglars? You know, one of you keeps the poor old soul talking on the doorstep, while the other goes round the back and helps himself to all her valuables. We were warned about it by that young policeman who looked as if he shouldn't be allowed out without his mum. He came to talk about crime prevention at our last Young Wives Group meetings.'

'If you mean a distraction burglary, then of course I'm not here for that,' Kat said indignantly. 'I — I just popped round for a chat, that's all.'

'A chat?' Elsie couldn't have looked more surprised if Kat had said she'd dropped in for a quick game of carpet bowls. 'What about?'

'Well, Jules was saying that she thought Gerald and Donald had had a bit of a set-to in the pub yesterday lunchtime. Is that right?'

Elsie looked at her, her head slightly on one side like a little bird, her eyes bright and inquisitive. 'Now, why would you want to know that?' she asked. 'Last week, you were quizzing me about Marjorie Hampton and now you're on about Mr High and Mighty Call-Me-Councillor Crabshaw. What is it with you?'

Kat shrugged. 'I was just curious, that's all.'

'Curious?' Elsie gave a cackle that would have done credit to the Wicked Witch of the West. 'You know what curiosity did, don't you?'

'Killed the cat?'

'And what were you insisting on people calling you the other day? Kat, was it?' Her face became suddenly serious, her eyes shrewd. 'You be careful, Katie. People get very funny when folk go around asking questions about them. And people aren't always what they seem, you know.'

'Who do you mean?'

'I'm naming no names. But let's just say, there are some people who don't like others prying into their business. They don't like it at all. And can get quite funny.'

That was rich, coming from Elsie, of all people. But Kat bit back the comment and merely nodded.

'Well, if you must know,' Elsie leaned forward, her eyes gleaming as they always did when she was about to pass on a particularly juicy bit of gossip, 'Donald said something to Gerald Crabshaw about paying his dues. At which, Gerald all but stamped his feet and left. Donald gave me one of those silly, embarrassed grins he does and said something about people who don't pay their bar bills and what makes them think he is made of money that he can extend them unlimited credit. Anyone would think there was Bank of Millford Magna over the front door, he said, the way some people took advantage of his good nature.'

So, not only was Gerald having an affair, he was running up debts. Kat felt a trickle of excitement. The evidence was stacking up fast against Gerald Call-Me-Councillor Crabshaw.

The question was: should she tell Sean before or after meeting Will for lunch? In the end, she decided to leave it until later. Sean was obviously busy today otherwise he'd have returned her earlier calls by now.

'Hurry along now,' Elsie smirked. 'You don't want to keep young Will Manning waiting, do you? If you ask me, you've been doing that for quite long enough.'

Kat stared at her. Centuries ago — she'd bet next month's salary on it if she had one — Elsie Flintlock would have been burned at the stake as a witch. 'How did you know I'm meeting Will?'

Elsie cackled. 'If you will hang about chatting on street corners, you must expect people to take notice.'

'You were in the minibus, weren't you?' she said as she remembered the one that had swept past as she'd waited to cross the road. 'But, I still don't see — '

'My friend Olive is a very good lip reader,' Elsie said as Kat's cheeks turned scarlet. 'And I don't think you're in a position to go around accusing folks of having a wagging tongue, do you? Now, you go off and meet your young man and forget all about asking questions. Like I said, people aren't always what they seem. He's not the empty-headed, harmless fool he appears to be.'

Before Kat could point out to Elsie that Will was not her 'young man' she'd closed the door. Kat stood on the doorstep for a few moments, thinking hard. So Elsie had seen this other side to Gerald Crabshaw, just as she had.

The question was: what to do about it?

15

'You ok?' Will asked, taking her hand as he helped her across the tumble of rocks on the edge of the beach.

'More than ok,' she breathed, filling her lungs with the crisp clean air. 'I'd forgotten how much I love it down here.'

Kat felt the tension she'd lived with for so long begin to ebb away as the salt-laden wind caught at her hair and blew away the last fragments of her disturbed night. Even the problem of what to do about her suspicions of Gerald Crabshaw faded for the moment. She'd call Sean about it later and see what he advised.

Millford Magna with its murder, gossip and intrigue seemed a million miles away as she and Will walked along the beach, their footsteps crunching on the shingle. It seemed the most natural thing in the world to remain hand in hand as they walked. Two good friends, enjoying each other's company. Nothing more.

'Let's see if you are still as rubbish at this as ever,' Will said as he sent a pebble skimming across the sea, skipping over the surface of the water like a swallow in flight.

'That's not fair. You've probably been practising,' Kat said as her pebble sank without trace after three pathetic bounces.

'Oh yes, of course. I get the chance to come down here most evenings — ' His sarcastic comment was cut off abruptly as a larger than expected wave caught him unawares, soaking his jeans from the knees down and leaving Kat helpless with laughter.

'Right. You've done it now. Prepare to be soaked.' Before she could run away, he grabbed her, pinned her arms to her sides and carried her down to the water's edge.

'No, please, Will, don't,' she screamed, kicking out in a futile attempt to free herself. 'These are my best jeans. They'll be ruined. Please. I'm begging you. Put me down. Please.'

He stopped, inches away from the sea and set her on her feet, although his arms were still around her. She looked up at him. She'd forgotten how tall he was, how lean and muscular, how safe she felt with his arms around her. Her breath caught in her throat.

'Will?' She must be seriously unfit if larking about on the water's edge for a couple of minutes left her feeling like she'd just run a marathon. 'We — we are all right now, you and me, aren't we?'

'How do you mean?' He sounded like he'd just run the marathon with her.

'I mean, we're still mates, aren't we?'

She staggered slightly on the damp shingle as he took his arms away. 'Yeah, we're still mates,' he said quietly, then with a complete change of tone called: 'Come on, race you to the cafe. Last one buys lunch.'

Over lunch, their conversation was light and undemanding with none of the awkward pauses there'd been earlier that morning. They agreed the sandwiches were even better than they remembered, the crab meat filling more succulent, the bread crustier. It was like the days out they used to have. Before things got complicated.

'Do you want a coffee?' Will asked as the leggy young waitress cleared their plates.

'Maybe later.' She stretched like a cat. 'Ah, that was so good. You're not in any rush to get back, are you?'

'No rush at all,' he smiled. 'In fact, there's something I want to say to you, Katie — no, sorry, don't bite my head off. I mean, Kat, of course. But do you have any idea how difficult it is to remember to call you that when I've known you all my life as Katie?'

'It doesn't matter,' Kat said, scanning the sweet menu and realising she couldn't eat another thing. 'I've almost given up trying to get people around here to do it. Are you having a sweet? The apple cake looks good.'

He shook his head. 'I'm done.'

'Me, too, more the pity. The thing is, Will, the longer I stay in Millford Magna, the less Kat and the more Katie I become.'

'And is that such a bad thing?' he asked, his face suddenly serious.

'In a way, yes. Katie is all about my

189

past. But Kat is my future.' And my future is anywhere but in Millford Magna, she wanted to add, but didn't. Instead, she settled for: 'I expect you think that sounds barmy?'

'Total nuts. But then, I always knew you were.' He picked up one of the small packets of sugar that were jammed into a glass in front of them and began to twist it between his fingers. When he looked up, Kat was surprised by the look of uncertainty in his eyes, like he was weighing up whether or not to say something and couldn't quite decide. 'You know how you said Dad and I aren't very good about talking about our feelings — '

He broke off as her phone began to ring. Kat glanced at it, The caller was Sean. Talk about bad timing. Whatever Will was trying to say, he'd be pretty mad if she interrupted him to take a call. She hit the button to send the call to voicemail.

'Anyone important?' Will asked.

'It was Sean,' she said, aware that Will's scowl seemed to be a knee jerk reaction to the very mention of Sean's name. 'I'll call him later. Now, what were you saying?

Something about you and your dad?'

'Well, not about him, really.' He concentrated on folding and refolding the sugar packet with clinical precision. 'I was — '

This time it was the ping of a text message that interrupted him. Once again, it was from Sean. It read: *Pls call me. URGENT.*

'I'm sorry, Will,' she said. 'Whatever it is, it sounds really important. I'll have to call him.'

Will pushed his chair back and stood up. 'It's ok,' he said stiffly. 'I'll go and get the coffee. You still take it black with a splash of milk and no sugar, I suppose?'

★ ★ ★

Sean answered at the first ring. 'What's so urgent that it can't wait until I've finished lunch?' Kat asked, trying but not quite succeeding in keeping a flash of irritation out of her voice.

'Did you tell anyone about following Doreen yesterday?' he asked, his voice low as if he was anxious not to be overheard. 'Anyone at all?'

'No. Why would I?'

'Then don't. Don't tell anyone.'

'Well, it's not something that's likely to come up in conversation, is it? But why? I don't understand — '

'I can't explain now. There's a big story breaking and I need to be there. In fact, I needed to be there ten minutes ago. Can you meet me tomorrow?'

'I'm not sure. I think Mum has got me enslaved for the rest of the week. But I'll see what I can do because there's something I need to talk to you about.'

Beyond the cafe window, she watched a group of seagulls swooping down low across the sea, filling the air with their shrill, mournful cries. It was like they were taunting her. She shivered as all her worries about Gerald Crabshaw came crowding back. So much for getting away from it all.

Sean gave an impatient sigh. 'Look, do you want this job or not?'

Kat sat up straight, excitement jolting through her. 'You mean a real job? With the Chronicle?'

'It's possible. Look, I've got to go. I'll

call you tomorrow about where and when to meet.'

'I'll be there, whatever suits you,' she said hurriedly 'I'll sort something with Mum. And Sean?'

'What?'

'Thanks. For thinking of me. For giving me a chance. That means a lot.'

'It's only a maybe. You do realise that, don't you?'

'Yes, but — '

'I'll call you tomorrow.'

★   ★   ★

'Good news?' Will said as he placed a steaming mug of coffee in front of her. 'You've got that smirk on your face you always get when you'd done something you're pretty pleased with.'

'I do not smirk.'

'Always have done. Ever since I've known you. In fact, we used to call you Smirker Latcham at school. Did you know that?'

'No you didn't. I refuse to believe that. Anyway, that's so unfair. I have nothing to smirk about. The job's anything but a done deal. Just a chance. A maybe is what Sean called it That's all.'

'What job?'

'Working for the Chronicle. Oh, Will, keep your fingers crossed for me. This is so what I want.'

'What, covering dog shows and parish council meetings? That's all there ever is in that blasted rag. Do you remember how we laughed that week when the lead story was about some washing being stolen from the launderette?'

'Don't you just wish that was this week's lead?' she said sombrely. 'It's not hard to guess what it's going to be.'

'Yeah right, so you're going to be the Chronicle's crime reporter, are you?'

'Of course I'm not, birdbrain. I know jolly well it's going to be dog shows and parish council meetings. But I don't mind. I loved the journalism part of my course and, though I say it myself, I was pretty good at it. This is it, Will, I can feel it. My ticket out of Millford Magna.'

'And is that so very important to you? To get away from Millford Magna?'

She sighed. 'It's ok for you. Your family is as much a part of this village as the duck pond. In fact, I dare say there were Mannings in Millford Magna when the Romans were rampaging around the country. You belong here. But I don't.'

'Now you're just being ridiculous,' he said. 'You belong here as much as I do.'

'But that's the thing. I don't anymore.' She inhaled the fragrant steam of the coffee and took a sip, her expression thoughtful as she tried to find the words that would make him understand how she felt. 'It's like — oh, I don't know. It's hard to put into words but, although I'll always love Millford Magna, it doesn't feel like my home anymore. When I look into my future, I don't see myself living here, married with two point four children, doing the school run, running the Play Group.'

'Would that be so bad? Jules seems happy enough.'

'But I'm not Jules. I want something different. I worked really hard at college, you know. I know you think I just racketed around the whole time, but I didn't. I want to be able to use it. That's why this job on the Chronicle is so important. As a stepping stone. Once I've got something like that on my CV, I'll be able to move on.'

'You've got it all worked out, haven't you?'

'I wish,' she said. 'But, that was the trouble with my job at the radio station. I didn't plan ahead enough. I should have started job hunting when I saw the warning signs and, looking back with the benefit of hindsight, there were plenty. If I'd done that, I'd have gone from one job straight into another, rather than wallowing about in the black hole of unemployment I'm in now. And the longer that gap is on my CV, the harder it will become. You do see that, don't you?'

'I suppose. Well, I'll keep my fingers crossed for you then,' he said.

'Thanks' She finished her coffee and pushed the empty cup to one side. 'Now, that's enough of me. What was it you wanted to tell me?'

He shook his head and lifted his jacket from the back of his chair. 'It was nothing important. Are you ready?'

'Ready for what? To beat you at pebble skimming? Because I have to warn you, William Edward Manning, I was letting you win earlier.'

'No, I meant ready to go,' he said, shrugging on his jacket, his face as dark as the bank of storm clouds that were building up out of sea.

She stared at him, perplexed by his abrupt change of mood. 'But I thought the plan was we were going to stay here for the afternoon? Maybe take a walk along the cliff path?'

'Sorry. I've got to get back. There's a million and one things to do on the farm. Besides, that rain is heading our way.'

He drove back to Millford Magna mostly in silence, only giving monosyllabic answers when pressed to do so until she finally got the hint and stopped trying to make conversation. And they said women were the moody ones, she thought. They'd obviously not met Will on one of his off days. He could make Mr Grumpy look like Little Miss Sunshine.

*   *   *

'You've got a bit more colour in your cheeks, love,' Cheryl said as Kat returned later that afternoon. 'All that fresh air must have done you some good But you're much earlier than I expected. I thought you were staying down the coast for most of the afternoon.'

'So did I,' Kat grumbled. 'But Will had to get back. Apparently, the farm can't survive without him.'

'Never mind. You're just in time for dinner. I've been trying out a new recipe.'

Kat's heart sank and her father, who had just come in, looked anxious.

'I thought Will brought you a leg of lamb this morning?' Kat said.

'I'm keeping that for Sunday. I think I'll invite your Nan over. She loves a nice Sunday roast. And maybe Will and John would like to come as well. What do you think?'

'Who knows?' Kat said gloomily. 'I've given up trying to work out what Will Manning does or doesn't like.' She lifted the lid of the saucepan and stared suspiciously at the pink sludgy mass while her father muttered something about getting a pie in the pub later. 'What is it?'

'It's a low carb beetroot risotto, which you make with cauliflower instead of rice,' Cheryl said brightly. 'It tastes better than it looks, honest.'

'Thanks, Mum, but I'll pass too. Will and I had a huge lunch. I'm still stuffed.'

'Well, I think that's — ' Cheryl began but broke off and looked anxiously at her daughter. 'Katie? Are you all right? You've gone as white as a sheet. What is it, love?'

Kat stood rigid with shock, her eyes wide, as she stared over her mother's shoulder at the television. The early evening local news had just started and there was a reporter standing in front of the blackened shell of a building.

'Oh yes, the fire. Nasty, wasn't it?' Cheryl said as she turned round to look. 'It was somewhere in Dintscombe although they didn't say exactly where. There was a bit about it on the lunchtime news. Apparently, the alarm was raised by a passing motorist in the early hours of this morning. But by the time the fire engine arrived, it was too late.'

'God, that's awful.'

'But that wasn't the worst of it. They found a body inside although they haven't identified it yet. I was trying to work out where the cottage was. What do you think? Looks as if it might be down by the park, if you wait for them to show a longer shot.'

But Kat didn't need to wait for the longer shot. She knew exactly where the burnt out cottage was. She should do. She'd spent enough time, the previous day, sitting in Cheryl's little pink car, staring at it. She also had a pretty good idea of the name of the casualty.

It was Doreen Spetchley's cottage. And it was, therefore, a safe bet that the body they found inside would be identified as that of Doreen Spetchley

16

'Katie? What is it?' Cheryl asked. 'Aren't you feeling well, love?'

The picture on the television switched to a report of a local football match and at last Kat was able to look away. Her mother's anxious voice barely penetrated the fog in her mind as she struggled to make sense of what she'd just seen.

'What is it?' Cheryl repeated. 'Come along, Katie. Speak to me. You're beginning to worry me, standing there like you've seen a ghost. Is it something on the telly? Something about the fire? Oh, love, is it someone you know? Is that it?'

Kat took a step back from the barrage of questions and shook her head. 'No. No. I didn't know her.'

'Her?' Cheryl frowned. 'How do you know it's a she? They said they hadn't identified the body yet.'

'No, of course not,' Kat said quickly. The last thing she wanted to do at that moment was tell her mother. At least, not until she'd spoken to Sean. She forced herself to calm down and think. 'But, face it, there's a fifty-fifty chance I'm right, isn't there? Sorry, but I've got to make a phone call.'

'But we're just about to eat.'

'I'm sorry. But I told you, Will and I had a huge lunch. I really couldn't eat a thing.'

And that was nothing but the truth. Even if her mother had been serving Will's lamb, cooked pink as she liked it with those lovely crunchy roast potatoes she did so well, Kat wouldn't have been able to force it down. She hurried out into the garden, well out of earshot, and keyed in Sean's number.

'Hi Kat. Sorry I had to cut you short earlier — '

'That doesn't matter. I've just seen the news on the television,' she said. 'About Doreen Spetchley. At least, I'm assuming it was her body they found in the fire.'

There was a slight pause. 'I'm afraid so. There has yet to be a formal identification. It's going to have to be done on dental records, unfortunately.'

Kat closed her eyes and shuddered. It was horrible to think of that tall, grey woman being only identifiable by her teeth. Horrible to think that the last time she'd seen her, she had been furiously angry — but very much alive.

'What happened?' she asked. 'Does anyone know?'

'An electrical fault, I imagine. It happened in the small hours of this morning so that's the most likely explanation. The only information the police will give is that their investigation is ongoing.'

'They said on the television that they're asking for anyone who saw anything to contact them. Do you think I should tell them about her meeting with Gerald Crabshaw?'

'But that was ages before the fire so can't have any relevance, can it?' he said. 'Besides, are you going to explain what you were doing spying on her? Following her? Because, I have to warn you, Kat, it's not going to look good on your CV. Not good at all.'

'But even so — '

'Trust me, Kat, you will achieve nothing by going to the police. Except subjecting yourself to a whole heap of awkward questions. Now, correct me if I'm wrong, but I would say that since finding Marjorie Hampton's body you've had enough of answering awkward questions, wouldn't you? It's up to you, of course. But my advice would be to say nothing. Because at the end of the day, there is nothing to say, is there?'

'No. I suppose not. But I wanted to tell you something about Gerald Crabshaw. He threatened me, you know.'

'He did what?'

'Said I was to stop poking my sticky little beak into his business. And he said it in exactly the same way he'd talked about Marjorie Hampton the day before she was killed. And, another thing, I happen to know that he has financial problems. And then, of course, there was the row that he had with Doreen Spetchley. It's all beginning to stack up against him, wouldn't you say?'

'What I would say, Kat, is that you should be very careful. This isn't a game of Cluedo, you know. This is the real thing. Two women have died.'

Kat's stomach lurched. 'You mean Doreen was murdered as well?'

'No, I don't. At the moment the police are treating her death as an accident, but what I'm trying to say is that somewhere out there is a very desperate person, someone who will stop at nothing to cover his — or her — tracks. Someone, too, who may not appreciate someone like you going around asking awkward questions. So, my advice to you is to forget all about Gerald Crabshaw.'

'But if he's guilty — '

'Then the police will deal with it. That's their job. And I might as well tell you, I'm putting my investigation into him on hold for the moment. At least until the police have finished looking into the fire. The last thing I want is to tread on their toes. And that's the last thing you want as well, trust me.'

'Yes, I take your point. To be honest, I'm more than a little relieved. The whole thing was beginning to give me nightmares. So, I suppose this means there's no point in us meeting up tomorrow now?'

'There's every point. Is eleven o'clock in the coffee shop in Dintscombe High Street convenient for you?'

'I'll be there,' she assured him. 'What sort of job are we talking about? It's not another surveillance job, is it?'

'I'll explain tomorrow. But I warn you, it has nothing to do with murder, corruption or anything like that. Something much more mundane, I'm afraid.'

With the image of the blackened wreckage of Doreen Spetchley's cottage still fresh in her mind, Kat reckoned she'd settle for mundane any day.

★   ★   ★

'I'm so sorry I'm late,' Kat said as she hurried into the Coffee Shop just before ten past eleven. 'The bus was late, then there are temporary traffic lights on the main road that took ages and — '

'It doesn't matter a bit.' Sean closed his laptop and stood up. 'I'll get you a coffee. You look as if you could do with one.

How do you like it?'

'Black with just a dash of milk and no sugar, please.' She watched him as he went up to the counter. Watched, too, the way other people — mostly women — watched him as well. So Sean thought she looked as if she could do with a coffee, did he? What was that supposed to mean? She resisted the urge to check her face in the mirror on the opposite wall. She looked a mess, she knew. The succession of sleepless nights she'd had were written in the dark circles under her eyes and the pallor of her skin.

Sean, on the other hand, looked amazing. There was an air of suppressed excitement about him, a sparkle in those clear grey eyes, like sunlit frost on a crisp winter day.

'So, how are you?' he said as he placed the coffee in front of her.

She shrugged. 'I've been better. I'm not sleeping too well at the moment. I keep thinking of Doreen. First Marjorie, now her, and I'm involved in some way with both. I think I must be jinxed.'

'Of course you're not. You just had the

bad luck of being in the wrong place at the wrong time. Now, as I said last night, I think the best thing to do is to forget all about that and concentrate on something different. That is, providing you were serious about becoming a journalist?'

'Of course I am. So what's this mysterious job? Is it another research assignment?'

He grinned. 'Nothing mysterious, I'm afraid. Just plain, boring, run of the mill stuff. There's a meeting of Millford Magna Parish Council tomorrow night and when I told Mike — that's the editor — about you, he was keen to let you have a go at covering it for us. You'll be paid lineage, that is, so much per line, at standard NUJ rates. It won't earn you a fortune but how about it?'

'That sounds great.' She thought how Will had teased yesterday about how the Chronicle was nothing but Parish Council Meetings and dog shows and couldn't wait to tell him. 'And the dog show? Would you like me to cover that too?'

'Is there one? Well, you can, if you like. It's up to you. What Mike is trying to do is get a network of village correspondents in the area, who report on things of interest in their own villages. You would be the first.'

'Village correspondent, eh? You mean, I'd be a sort of Kate Adie?'

'In a way, although I have to say, you're a whole lot better looking than her.'

Suddenly, Kat forgot the rings under her eyes, the pallor of her skin. If Sean thought she looked ok, that was good enough for her. 'I can't thank you enough, Sean,' she said. 'I'll do a good job, I promise.'

'Sure, I know you will. And I'll be around if you need any help. As for thanking me, you can do that by holding your nerve and not to be saying anything about Sunday. If it gets out that I asked you to put Doreen Spetchley under surveillance, that'll be my job on the line as well as yours. Ever since the phone hacking scandal, Mike has been as jumpy as a kitten about anything that smacks of press intrusion.'

★　★　★

Kat left her bike propped against the school wall and checked her bag for the third time that evening. Notebook, pen, spare pen. That, according to Sean, was all she needed. That and a whole heap of confidence.

It seemed strange to be walking across the school playground and even stranger to see that the climbing bars were still there, although the surface beneath them was now a strange rubbery one rather than the bone crunching tarmac that had been there when she'd swung from above as a child. There, too, were the lines marking out a game of hopscotch and, for one second, she was tempted to see if she could still do it.

She was so pleased she resisted the temptation as, seconds later, she heard someone come in to the playground from the car park.

'You.' Gerald Crabshaw stood, holding on to the gate, his face contorted with anger at the sight of her. 'What the devil are you doing here? You're following me again.'

'How can I be following you?' Kat said,

sounding a lot more courageous than she felt. 'I was here before you. I could accuse you of following me.'

'What are you doing here?' he scowled.

'If you must know, I'm here for the Parish Council Meeting,' she said. 'I'm covering it for the Chronicle.'

'What?' He gave a short laugh that was more of a sneer. 'You? Working for the Chronicle? Barmaid to journalist in one day, eh? Well, your new job won't last any longer than the previous one. I'll see to that. I'm a personal friend of Mike Chalmers and I'll be having a word with him. This is harassment, that's what it is.'

'What's going on here, Gerald? Is something wrong?' A tall, white-haired man, who Kat recognised as a retired solicitor who lived in the High Street, came up behind them. She'd done her homework and knew his name was Stuart Davies and that he was the Chairman of the Parish Council.

Gerald whirled round. 'Good to see you, Stuart. I was just sending this — this person on her way.'

'Are you here for the meeting?' Stuart

smiled kindly at Kat, who nodded. Then he turned to Gerald. 'Members of the public are welcome to attend council meetings, as Councillor Crabshaw well knows,' he said.

'Oh, I'm not a member of the public. I'm from the Chronicle,' Kat said quickly and couldn't resist adding: 'I'm the newly appointed Village Correspondent for Millford Magna.'

'Are you indeed? How splendid. Come along in.'

'If she goes in, I won't,' Gerald Crabshaw said, his voice bristling with scarcely contained anger.

Stuart turned to face him, his expression bland. 'That's your choice entirely, Councillor Crabshaw. As you know, as our District Councillor, you are always welcome to attend our meetings. So, too, are members of the Press. Now, shall we go in?'

Gerald Crabshaw swore, turned round and stalked off in the direction of the car park.

'I'm sorry,' Kat said. 'I don't want to cause trouble — '

'Don't worry. You haven't. To be perfectly frank, my dear, the chap is a complete pain in the you-know-where. But that's strictly off record, ok? I'm delighted that we're finally going to get our meetings covered in the Chronicle, if only to let people know what we as a council do and, hopefully, to get more of them involved. So, come on in and I'll introduce you to the Clerk. She's the one who does the real work around here.' He opened the door for her, ushered her in and added in a low voice, 'Be prepared to be bored rigid.'

In fact, Kat was nothing of the sort. She was so busy taking notes, trying to keep track of who said what, that the hour and a half meeting flew by in no time as the pages of her notebook filled up nicely.

★ ★ ★

The next morning, Kat was sitting at her laptop, the notes from the previous night's meeting, some of which were completely undecipherable, spread out in front of her. Her head was aching from

213

trying to remember the things Sean had told her and she wished she'd had the sense to write them down at the time. He'd started off by saying something about what not to do. What was it? Don't write the report of the whole meeting in one chunk. Break it down into a number of separate stories.

That was it. That way, he'd said, it made it easier to read, not to mention the fact that it would earn her more in lineage.

Then there were those questions she had to ask each time. She should have remembered them from her journalism module at college but that had been a long time ago. What were they now? Something like who, what, where, when and why?

After a few abortive attempts, she began to produce what she hoped was acceptable copy and was into her third story, an account of complaints that had been received about overgrown footpaths which she thought she might talk to Sean about, to see if she should do a follow-up, when Cheryl called up the stairs.

'Katie? Will you come down here, please? Now?'

Her voice had that she-who-must-be-obeyed quality about it that made Kat sigh, hit the save button and close her laptop. She looked at her watch. The eleven o'clock shampoo and set must have arrived early.

'Katie?' Cheryl's voice had a strange edge to it that Kat couldn't identify. She sounded pretty stressed, that was for sure. 'Are you coming? There's someone to see you.'

Kat hurried down the stairs — and stopped dead, a sick feeling in the pit of her stomach. A policeman, who looked as if he was more at home on a rugby pitch than in her mum's tiny kitchen, turned as she came into the room.

'Are you Kathryn Latcham?' he asked.

'Yes. Well, Kat actually. Or I even answer to Katie sometimes. If I have to. Although I prefer Kat.' She was talking too fast. Talking too much. Talking rubbish. Frantically trying to get her brain in gear.

'Were you driving a pink Fiat Panda in Dintscombe on Sunday afternoon. Vehicle

215

registration number — '

As he reeled off the numbers, Cheryl's face paled and she looked anxiously at Kat. 'That's my car, officer,' she said. 'And Katie was driving it with my consent. Is there a problem?'

'If you don't mind, Mrs Latcham, I'd prefer it if your daughter answered the questions. Were you driving that particular car in Dintscombe on Sunday afternoon?'

Kat nodded, hoping against hope she'd been captured on CCTV going through a red light or something. 'Yes.' Her voice came out as a high-pitched squeak.

The policeman moved forward and Kat took an instinctive step backwards. 'Then would you care to explain what you were doing, parked outside a house in Park Road, Dintscombe, for over an hour on Sunday? A house which has subsequently burnt to the ground?'

17

Kat stared at the bulky policeman as her brain turned to porridge and her legs to jelly. She put out a hand to grab the back of the nearest chair. What to do? What to say? The only thing she could think of was Sean, warning her that his job, as well as hers, would be on the line if the editor found out that he'd asked her to watch Doreen Spetchley that afternoon.

'I'm sorry. I didn't quite get that,' she said, playing for time in the hope that her brain would start working again. 'What was I doing where?'

'In Park Road, Dintscombe.' He didn't quite succeed in hiding his impatience. 'The lay-by just outside the entrance to the park. Your car was seen there.'

'My mother's car,' she quickly corrected him before Cheryl could. 'But, yes, I remember now. Of course I do. I'd stopped to take a phone call. After all, that's what we are told to do, aren't we?

Not to answer our phones while we are driving. Which of course I don't. Ever. So — so when this call came in, I pulled in to take it.'

'Really?' He lifted one dark, heavy brow and Kat couldn't help wondering if he spent hours in front of the mirror practising that particular yeah-yeah-I've-heard-that-one-before look. 'It must have been a pretty long phone call. According to our information, you were parked there for well over an hour.'

'I was?'

He nodded. 'According to a very security conscious neighbour. He became so suspicious about the length of time you were there that he took the trouble to take a note of your registration number as well as a very accurate description of the vehicle.'

'I admit I stopped there for a few minutes, but I wouldn't have thought it was that long. Maybe there was another car that came along when he wasn't looking. I can't believe he sat at his window watching me for a whole hour. That would have been bonkers.'

'Indeed. But how many other bright pink cars are there in the area with 'Chez Cheryl' painted down the side?'

She shook her head. What did she do now? Hold out her wrists and say something like 'It's a fair cop'?

'Exactly,' he said. 'Now, shall we start again? What were you doing, parked in the lay-by for over an hour on Sunday afternoon?'

Kat sighed and rubbed the back of her neck. 'Well, if you must know,' she said with what she hoped was a sheepish grin. 'It's all a bit embarrassing and silly. I was following a lead I'd been given. I'm a journalist, you see.'

Behind her, she heard Cheryl's sharp intake of breath and prayed she wouldn't say anything.

'In that case, may I see your press card?'

'Well, the thing is, I don't actually have one yet. I'm very new. I haven't been there very long and I'm on probation, as it were. Particularly as the rest of them in the news room are concerned. I think one of them was having a bit of a joke with me. Gave me a tip off that a famous footballer was going to be in Dintscombe Park on Sunday afternoon. The rumour was he was having an affair with some local girl and if I got lucky, I could maybe get a picture of them.'

'And which famous footballer would that be?' He had another look now. One that said 'And I don't believe that one either'.

'Do you know, I honestly can't remember his name. I'm not really into footballers. Rugby's more my thing. Although I've got it and his picture, obviously. How else would I know who I was looking at? It's all in my notes, which are upstairs. I can go and check it out, if you like,' she offered, hoping that if he took her up on it she'd have time to google famous footballers and grab a name.

'Don't bother,' he said.

'I feel really stupid about the whole thing now,' she rushed on, anxious to make herself sound as embarrassed and foolish as possible. 'I mean, I should have checked my sources more carefully, I realise that now. But I was told it was all hush, hush and that it was my big chance to make a name for myself. How naive was I? Sitting there for over an hour. Looking at nothing in particular and bored out of my mind. I bet they've had a really good laugh about it back in the office.'

Kat was hugely relieved to see him smother a grin. 'I think you do, indeed, need to check your sources more carefully next time,' he said. 'But while you were there, waiting for your famous footballer, did you happen to notice anyone visiting the cottage opposite?'

'You mean, the one that burned down?' Kat's eyes widened. 'Wasn't that a terrible thing to happen?'

'Did you see anyone?' he repeated without making an attempt to answer her question.

'No. Only the lady who lived there. At least I suppose it was her. She came out while I was waiting there, got into her car and drove off. Oh Lord, was it her body they found in the fire?'

Again, he ignored the question. 'You say you saw her? What time was this?'

'It would have been about half past three. She drove off in the direction of the High Street.' She stopped herself from adding that she didn't know where she went after that. She'd already told one outright lie and a couple of half truths. She didn't fancy racking up any more.

He handed her a card. 'Well, if you think of anything else, perhaps you'd contact me on that number?'

'Of course.'

As Cheryl went to let him out, Kat sat down in the nearest chair with a thump as her legs finally gave way.

'Well, what was all that about?' Cheryl asked as she came back. 'Famous footballer, indeed. You wouldn't know a famous footballer from Mickey Mouse. What's going on, Katie? What were you really doing in Dintscombe on Sunday? Was it something to do with that poor woman who got killed in that fire? Come on. Out with it. Time for some answers, young lady, don't you think?'

'Later, Mum. I'll tell you later, I promise. But first I must make a phone call.'

At that moment, the door into the salon pinged. 'You're going nowhere, except into the salon and shampooing Mrs. Tinley,' Cheryl said firmly. 'That's her now. Go on. We'll finish this little chat later. I don't know what you're up to, Katie, but whatever it is, it's giving me a very bad feeling.'

★   ★   ★

It was over an hour before Kat got the chance to slip away from her mother's ever watchful eye on the pretext of getting a fresh batch of towels from the airing cupboard. As soon as she was out of earshot she called Sean.

'I had a visit from the police,' she said quietly the second he answered. 'Apparently, I was seen on Sunday.'

'The devil you were!' he exclaimed angrily. 'Did I not tell you not to follow her?'

'Yes, you did,' she said, stung by his sharp tone into speaking louder than she'd meant to. She lowered her voice again, not wanting her mother to hear.

'And, for your information, I was seen by one of her neighbours when I was parked in the lay-by, not when I was following her. And don't worry, I kept your name out of it.'

'I am so sorry, Kat, I surely am,' he said, his voice back to its normal lilting Irish cadences. 'I didn't mean to bark at you. I was worried about you, that was all.'

Kat suppressed the retort that it had sounded rather more like he'd been worried about himself, not her, as he went on with that soft, sexy laugh that sent shivers down her back: 'And if you will insist on driving a car that looks like a marshmallow on wheels, I'm not surprised you were seen. You can't say I didn't warn you.'

That sexy laugh also made her forget she was supposed to be annoyed with him as she, too, laughed. 'You did indeed. Well, apparently, a neighbour saw me parked in the lay-by, got suspicious and took down my registration number.'

'So what did you tell the police?'

She groaned at the memory. 'I had to

think quickly. I said I'd been given a tip-off that a famous footballer was meeting a local girl in the park — and that I'd found out later that the tip-off was a wind-up from someone in the office.'

'And which famous footballer would that be?' he asked, echoing almost word for word the question the policeman had asked.

'I don't know. I only said footballer because Dad had left the paper on the table, open at the sports pages. I'm not much of a football fan and the only one I could think of at that moment was David Beckham, which I didn't think would work. So I said I couldn't remember his name and offered to go upstairs and find it, in the hope that while I was out of the room I could google something. Luckily, he believed me. Or at least, he believed I was stupid enough to fall for a wind-up like that. I told him how I'd just started at the Chronicle and how keen I was to make a name for myself.'

'Ah yes, now,' Sean said slowly. 'About that. I've been meaning to call you all morning but there hasn't been a chance.

I'm afraid there's a problem.'

'What sort of problem?' Even as she asked the question, Kat had the uncomfortable feeling she wasn't going to like the answer.

'Mike called me into his office this morning. It appears he's having second thoughts about the whole idea of using Village Correspondents. Or Community Correspondents as he was going to call them, as he thought it sounded more inclusive. He was really taken with the idea. But that was yesterday. Now today, he's had a change of heart and thinks it could create problems.'

Kat's stab of disappointment was like a physical pain. 'What sort of problems?' she hissed, trying to remember to keep her voice down.

'He didn't say. And why are you whispering?'

'Because I don't want my mother to hear. I'm in enough trouble with her as it is. I'm supposed to be fetching some towels and she'll be yelling up the stairs for me any moment.'

'Then you'd better go.'

'No. I need to know about my job. Or lack of it. This is down to Gerald Crabshaw again, isn't it? You said the other day that he and your editor exchange funny handshakes which I take it means they both belong to the same mutual backscratching club. In fact, only last night Gerald boasted about getting me fired from not one but two jobs.'

'Last night? How do you mean?'

'At the Parish Council meeting. I turned up, as agreed and he was the first person I saw. He told me to go home.'

'So you didn't cover the meeting? Well, at least that was one good thing. I would hate to think you'd done that for nothing.'

'But of course I covered the meeting. As a matter of fact, the chairman came along and insisted that I did so. Gerald did this 'either she goes or I do' thing and went off in high dudgeon. I tell you, Sean, I am so not his favourite person at the moment.'

Sean sighed. 'Did I or did I not tell you to keep away from him?'

'And I did. It wasn't my fault he turned

up for the meeting last night, was it?'

'No. I suppose not. But trouble does seem to follow you around like the proverbial bad penny, Kat. Maybe it's best you forget about this job, at least until things settle down.'

'But that's so unfair,' she protested. 'None of this is my fault. Besides, I've already written up two pieces from last night's meeting and am about to start on a third about the footpath obstructions. The Chairman's going to think it pretty odd if, having made a point of insisting that I stay and cover the meeting, my stories don't appear, isn't he?'

'Katie?' Cheryl's voice came up the stairs. 'What are you doing up there, for goodness sake? Mrs Marshall is waiting for her coffee. Black, two sugars. Not too strong.'

'Sorry, Mum. Just coming,' Kat called, then went back to Sean: 'I've got to go.'

'OK. And Kat, I think you're absolutely right. Stuart Davies would find it pretty odd if the stories didn't appear. You go ahead, write them up and email them in. I'll square it with Mike. Would you like to email them to me first and I'll give them the once over, then forward them for you?'

'Would you? That would be brilliant. Thanks, Sean, you're a star,' she breathed, suddenly lightheaded with relief. 'Do you know, this is the second time Gerald Crabshaw has tried to get me sacked. I must have got him really rattled again, just like that time in the pub when I asked him where he was the day Marjorie was killed. If you could have seen his face when he saw me last night. Talk about if looks could kill. He — oh, my God.'

The pile of warm towels in her hand felt like ice as a chill ran through her body.

★   ★   ★

'Kat? What's wrong?'

'I — I've just remembered something. Something that will prove he was lying about his alibi. Gerald Crabshaw killed Marjorie Hampton, Sean, and I think I can prove it.'

'What on earth — ?'

229

'No, I've got to go. Mum will be sending out a search party if I don't. And besides, I need to think this through and check a few things out before I say any more. Check my sources, like a good journalist should. Isn't that what you told me?'

'Indeed I did. But I also told you to be very careful. Gerald Crabshaw's a nasty piece of work. Not that I'm saying he's a murderer, mind you. But he's definitely hiding something, the very least of which is his affair with Doreen Spetchley. Something that, after this latest news, he'll be even more anxious to cover up.'

'How do you mean?'

'I've just come from a police press conference. They don't think Doreen's death was an accident. The post mortem showed she was dead before the fire started. Now, if you're right about Crabshaw, there's no saying what he'd do if you challenged him. Promise me you won't.'

'Don't worry. It's not Gerald I'm going to see. But someone who can prove that he was lying about his alibi. And then I'll go to the police.'

'Look, we need to get together and talk this through before you do that. I'm tying up a few things here then I'll be on my way to Millford Magna anyway. I've been trying all morning to get hold of Gerald Crabshaw to interview him but have drawn a blank every time and I'm just hoping he hasn't done a bunk. So promise me that if you do see him, you won't approach him, follow him or antagonise him in any way but will contact me. I'd hate to think you'd blundered in and scared him off.'

Blundered in? She drew in a sharp breath. What did he think she was? 'Of course I wouldn't blunder in as you put it,' she said indignantly. 'I'm not a fool, you know.'

'That's your opinion,' he snapped, then went on quickly before she could protest. 'And I don't need to remind you, do I, that Gerald Crabshaw is my story? And it's very unprofessional of one journalist to pinch another's story.'

'But I wasn't — ' she tried to interrupt but he wouldn't let her.

'In fact, to put it bluntly,' he said sharply, no trace of that lovely Irish warmth in his voice any more, 'this is my big chance, Kat, my ticket out of this hell-hole and I'll not have it wrecked by a little girl like you playing at being a journo. So keep out of it. Go back to your little old ladies and their perms and leave the real work to the professionals. Do you understand?'

Before she had the chance to come back with some withering put-down, he ended the call.

18

Kat was shaking with anger as she put her phone back in her pocket. What a low-life. He'd used her all the way along, first because he thought she'd give him all the gory details about finding Marjorie's body and then later when he needed someone to watch Doreen Spetchley's house. And to think she'd covered up for him by not telling the police what she was really doing outside Doreen's house on Sunday.

'Katie?' Cheryl's voice was sharper this time. 'Are you coming? Mrs Marshall would like her coffee this morning, not tomorrow.'

As Kat went back into the salon she was in a quandary. She wanted to go and see Jules before she left for her lunchtime shift at the Mucky Duck. But if she told her mother she had to go out urgently, then she'd want to know why and would make a fuss. Maybe even insist on having that 'little chat' she threatened her with earlier.

On the other hand if she made out her visit to Jules was merely a social one, then Cheryl would just keep finding her jobs to do and she'd be here for the rest of the day.

Eventually, it was almost half past one by the time she got away on the pretext of meeting Jules to arrange a girlie night out. She got her bike out of the shed and was about to get on and pedal off in the direction of the High Street when she heard the throaty roar of a powerful car coming down the road towards her. Her heart sank.

It was Gerald Crabshaw, the last person in the world she wanted to see. For a moment, she considered turning round and going back home but while she was dithering, he stopped his car in the middle of the road and jumped out.

'Katie. You're just the person I was hoping to see,' he called as he walked towards her.

And you're just the person I was hoping not to see, Kat could have said but didn't. Instead she gave him a false bright smile. 'I'm so sorry,' she called, pulling the bike round so that it faced in the other direction. 'I — I can't stop. I really am in the most terrible rush. I'm late as it is.'

With a turn of speed she'd never have thought him capable of, he hurried towards her and, before she realised his intentions, reached out and put both hands on her handlebars. She was stuck, straddled across the bike, one foot on the floor, the other on her pedal and could do nothing or go anywhere. She looked around, desperately. Who would see her? Or hear her if she yelled? The days when people stood around gossiping on the streets of Millford Magna were long gone, along with the shops and post office.

'Look,' he said, in a soft, almost hesitant tone of voice she'd never heard him use before. 'I'm sorry if I startled you. I just wanted to apologise for last night at the Parish Council meeting. I don't know what came over me, I really don't. I'd had some bad news, a dear friend of mine tragically killed, but even so, there was no excuse for taking it out on you. I'm deeply, deeply sorry.'

Gerald Crabshaw apologising? Had she wandered into a parallel universe by mistake? There'd be a squadron of pigs flying overhead next.

'That's ok really. There's nothing to apologise for,' she said hastily. 'Now, if you'll excuse me, I really am late.'

'I won't keep you. I just came to see if I could make it up to you a bit,' he said. 'Forget last night's Parish Council meeting with its boring little bits about pot-holes and missing cats' eyes. I've got a story for you that could well turn out to be the scoop of the century. Isn't that what you journalists say?'

'Well, actually, the editor is having second thoughts about employing me, thanks to you.'

'Then this is my way of making it up for you and, don't worry, I'll talk to Mike. Trust me, Katie, this will be a big one, front page of the nationals. Mike will be desperate to take you on but this will get your CV out there. You'll be able to take your pick.'

'It sounds great, but — '

'Look, I know we got off on the wrong foot, but how about we meet up later and I give you all the gen and you can make up your own mind what you do about it? I've just got to pop into Dintscombe then I'll be dropping in to the Mucky Duck for a quick one. Why don't we meet in there in, say, half an hour?'

Kat was about to say no way, or something like that, when she stopped and thought about what he'd said. She looked at him closely. Certainly there was none of the usual swaggering bluster about him today. In fact, he looked as if he'd shrunk since last night. His eyes had a vacant, soft-focussed look, his skin pale and sallow.

What harm could it possibly do? And if she could get one over on Sean after what he'd said, then so much the better. And it would do no harm to her standing with Mike, the editor, would it?

Suddenly, Gerald scowled and jerked on the handlebars so hard she almost overbalanced. 'For heaven's sake, girl, what's to think about?' he said, his voice harsh, his eyes no longer soft focussed and vague but hot and angry and glaring directly at her. 'I suppose the story is not enough for you, is that it? You want money as well?'

'What do you mean? I don't — '

'You saw us, didn't you? Up in Compton Woods.'

Kat backed away as far as she could without falling over, flustered by his sudden change of tone. Gone was the penitent, apologetic man. In his place, the arrogant pushy one she knew so well. Once again, she looked around her at the deserted village street.

'I — I don't know what you mean, honest,' she said quickly, her heart thumping against her ribcage. 'And why would I want money? If I had seen something up in Compton Wood, which I didn't, I swear, I wouldn't say anything, I promise, least of all try to blackmail you. Look, I must go. My friend will be wondering where I am and start sending out search parties.'

'You'd better not say anything,' he snarled, now reverted completely to type, 'else it will be the worse for you.'

She was scared, of course she was. But there was something about the way he spoke that lit a fuse in her so that, for a moment at least, she forgot her fear and felt only blind reckless fury as she remembered Marjorie and Doreen.

'Oh right,' she flashed. 'Is that how you deal with everyone who gets in your way? First, Marjorie and now Doreen. How could you do that to someone you pretended to be fond of?'

'Don't be ridiculous. You can't think I had anything to do with either death. Besides, Doreen's was just a horrible accident.'

'That's not what the police are saying,' Kat said.

'Oh and of course, I'm forgetting, you have a direct line to the police, don't you?' he sneered.

'I have my sources,' she said. 'And they are saying that Doreen Spetchley did not die in the fire. Suspicious circumstances, the police are saying. Apparently, she was dead before the fire started.'

Gerald's face went from white to grey

and through all fifty shades in between. He stepped back from the bike as if the handlebars had suddenly become searing hot and stared at Kat, with the half desperate, half spoiling-for-a-fight look of a cornered rat.

Kat took her chance, pulled the bike towards her and pedalled off as fast as she could, the anger that had given her that little spurt of courage now evaporated.

'Katie, come back.' Gerald shouted after her but Kat wasn't hanging around to ask him why. Her only thought was to get away from him and into a place where there were other people around as quickly as possible.

★   ★   ★

Kat felt a moment of panic as she thought at first the bar was empty. Then she heard the sound of chinking glasses and saw that Jules was stacking glasses in the dishwasher while from the back kitchen came the reassuring sound of Donald, banging around.

'Blimey, Kat, you look like you did that

day we got chased by John Fleming's bull.' Jules looked at her anxiously. 'What's wrong?'

'I just had a rather unpleasant encounter with Gerald Crabshaw. He's quite mad, you know. Completely bonkers. And what's more I'm pretty damn sure I've got proof that he killed Marjorie.'

'You're kidding,' Jules's eyes widened. 'What sort of proof?'

'Do you remember that day you were late picking Kylie up from school? The day Marjorie Hampton was killed?'

'I should do. Her teacher still hasn't forgiven me.'

'And why did you say you were late?'

'The main road was closed by an accident for most of the afternoon and the bus had to go around all the villages. It took forever.'

'Exactly. Don't you see? Donald and Gerald were each other's alibis. One of them, I can't remember which, said they were at a meeting about the site of possible new playing fields out on the bypass that day. But you see, they couldn't have been because the road was closed. There was no way they could have got there. They were lying — and it's my bet that Gerald has something on Donald to force him to back up his story. That's why Gerald got me sacked from the pub. I think that was the first story they came up with and it was only later they realised the road was closed and then had to change it to something else.'

Jules's looked shocked. 'God, Kat, what are you going to do about it?'

'Tell the police, of course. I think they'd be very interested in the fact that our Councillor Crabshaw lied about his whereabouts the day Marjorie Hampton was killed, don't you?'

Before Jules could say anything, Donald rushed into the bar, his expression grave.

'Julie, I'm so sorry,' he said. 'That was the school on the phone just now. I'm afraid your Kylie's had an accident. Only a bit of a bump on the head, they say. Nothing to worry about, but they say they think you should come and take her home. That she'll be — '

But before he could deliver the rest of the message, Jules was gone, leaving the

242

door wide open behind her. Donald walked across and closed it.

★ ★ ★

'Poor Julie,' he murmured. 'Children are such a worry, aren't they? Always in to something. I must say, I'm quite glad that Joyce and I were never blessed.'

'Yeah, poor Jules. She looked frightened to death.'

'Well, I'm sure little Kylie will be fine.' Donald carried on loading the dishwasher where Jules had left off. 'I couldn't help but overhear your conversation just now, what with the pub being so quiet.'

And you straining your ears to hear, Kat could have added. But didn't.

'Publicans do a lot of that, you know. Overhearing things you weren't meant to.' Donald had finished stacking the dishwasher and leaned across the bar, looking as if he was settling down for a chat. 'Sometimes people act as if you're not there, you know. I've heard them going on about me being the grey man, taking the mick about how Joyce shouts at me, things like that. Sometimes, I can be stood right there by the bar. But they just don't notice me.'

'I'm sorry — ' Kat had no idea what she was apologising for, but she felt Donald was expecting one. The last thing she wanted him to do right now was to tell her the pub was closing and turf her out, in case Gerald was still hanging around.

'You know, I've had my suspicions of Gerald Crabshaw for some time now, same as you have.' Donald reached down behind the counter and took out a bottle and two glasses. 'You're looking a bit pale, Katie. Would you like a drink? I'm having one.'

'No. I don't — ' she began, then thought again about Gerald waiting for her outside. 'Yes, a drink would be fine. A glass of dry white wine, please.'

'You need something stronger than that. You look like you've had a shock. Try this. It's my favourite single malt whisky. Definitely not for the customers.' He poured the peaty brown liquid into a glass and handed it to her.

Kat shrugged and took the glass. She raised it to her lips and coughed slightly as the fumes hit the back of her throat. 'Strong stuff,' she murmured, her eyes watering.

'Sip it slowly,' he said with a smile. 'You're supposed to be savouring it.'

Kat took a sip and smiled back. Donald wasn't such a bad chap, after all. 'You were saying about Gerald Crabshaw,' she prompted. 'That you had your suspicions about him. What sort of suspicions?'

'The worst. He really is a nasty piece of work, you know, and if you have evidence against him that the police can use to put him away, then that's great. You were absolutely right about that so-called alibi I gave him as being false, you know. Luckily, the police didn't ask me for one, else I would be in all sorts of trouble now, wouldn't I? And goodness knows what Joyce would say if she came back from her cruise to find I was in trouble with the police. Publicans have to be very careful, you know.'

'Yes, I suppose you do. But why did you do it?'

'Simple. Gerald was blackmailing me over something that happened as a result of some minor bookkeeping errors. So when I had these little temporary difficulties I was foolish enough to confide in him and he lent me some money to sort it out. And, like a fool, I accepted. He says he will demand immediate repayment and report me to the Inland Revenue if I don't back his story up about the day Marjorie Hampton was killed. Well, I'll be honest, I thought I was just covering up for one of these countless affairs he's always having and went along with it. I know what I did was wrong. But he's a very forceful man.'

'The — the guy's a first class rat,' I said, lifting my glass. 'Cheers.'

'Cheers. Is the whisky helping? I must say, you're a much better colour now. You were quite pale before.'

'Yes. I'm feeling much better, thanks. I could get a taste for this stuff.'

Donald smiled briefly, then looked anxious again. 'Of course, now I don't think it was an affair he was asking me to cover for but something much worse. I think he killed Marjorie Hampton. And I don't mind telling you, Katie, the whole thing has been giving me nightmares. I wake up most nights, sweat running down my face, the image of that poor soul, with her legs stuck up in the air — '

Kat stopped, the glass half way to her lips. 'How did you know?' she asked.

'How did I know what?'

'That she was found with her legs stuck up in the air. As far as I know, the police haven't released that bit of information.'

'Oh Lord, is that right?' He nibbled the back of his thumb, his thin, grey face creased with worry. 'Well, Gerald told me of course. Which kind of proves beyond doubt that he's the murderer, wouldn't you say? What do you think we should do?'

'Tell the police, of course.' It was no comfort to Kat to be proved right. There was something seriously weird about finding that someone you've known all your life is a cold-blooded murderer. 'Gerald tried to trap me, you know. He wanted me to meet him here in the bar at closing time. Said he had a really big story that was going to get my byline on the front page of the nationals. I imagine that, had I fallen for it, there'd have been some sort of 'accident' before I got here.'

'But you didn't fall for it?'

'What? His scoop of the century story? Of course not. It was just a ploy to get me here.'

He smiled. 'Very wise. But why don't we play him along with that one and see where it leads us? You never know, he might give us something we can take to the police.'

'But I've already told him no.'

'Don't worry. I'll get him to come here. I'll spin him some story that will bring him here. Now, finish your drink. I don't want him coming in and seeing us getting cosy over a drink together.'

'But this is a pub. It's not unusual for people to be having a drink together.'

'Yes, but Gerald's cute enough to know that this malt is something I don't sell but only give to special customers. If he sees you drinking it, it'll make him suspicious. So, are you up for it?'

Kat didn't like the idea of coming face to face with Gerald Crabshaw again but she very much liked the idea of the net closing in on the monster who murdered those two poor women. She was up for it.

19

'OK then,' Donald said. 'I'll just go and phone Gerald. But are you quite sure you're all right about this? You're looking a bit peaky. Maybe this isn't such a good idea after all.' His thin face was pinched with indecision and anxiety. 'Why don't we simply forget about the whole thing and call the police? If Gerald squirms his way out of it, so be it. Better that than put yourself in danger. Even though it means everyone will know what a fool I was and you lose the big 'how I helped bring a vicious killer to justice' story. But you'll still have plenty to write about, won't you? And most people think I'm a fool anyway, so nothing would have changed there.'

Kat was feeling more than a bit peaky and desperately in need of some fresh air. Even so, those headlines were very tempting and Sean's 'amateur' jibe still smarted. 'It seems a shame, though, when we're so close,' she murmured.

'You're right. It does seem a shame.' He frowned and looked deep in thought for a moment. 'Look, I'll tell you what I'll do. I'll lock the front door and tell him to come around the back. That way, he won't catch you unawares.' He crossed the bar and locked the front door. 'How about that? He'll come in to the bar through the kitchen and he won't even see me, tucked behind here. What do you think? There's no way he'll get past me to get to you.'

Kat swallowed against the wave of nausea that rose in her throat. Was she being stupid? Should she call the whole thing off, as Donald suggested? Or maybe phone Will and ask him to meet her here? But if she did that, he'd insist on knowing why and would tell her not to do it and let the police handle it. And she had no intention of phoning Sean. Ever again.

On the other hand, if she could hold her nerve she could be in on the ground floor of the biggest story of the century. And wouldn't that put Sean's nose out of joint? He wouldn't be able to accuse her of blundering around like an amateur ever again.

'I think that could work well,' she said with a confidence she was far from feeling, 'I just had a bit of a wobble, that's all. Gerald was pretty damn mad just now. I don't mind admitting, he scared me.'

'I can imagine. Look, does this make you feel any better? I call it my security blanket.' Donald reached down to a shelf below the counter and brought up a battered-looking baseball bat. He held it with one hand and ran the other over it, smoothing the long slender trunk as if it was a finely tuned musical instrument. 'I've never used it, either on or off a baseball pitch, but I feel safer just knowing it's there. I always keep it down here, in case things get rowdy.'

Kat couldn't help smiling at the thought of meek and mild Donald — who, according to the wags among the early evening crowd, was so afraid of his own shadow he wouldn't go out on a sunny day — running around a group of rowdy customers, brandishing a baseball bat. She shook her head. It was no good, she simply couldn't imagine it. But if he was up for it, then so was she. 'OK then. Let's do it.'

'Trust me, Katie, I'll be just behind here all the time. I'll see he doesn't lay a finger on you, I promise.'

Kat suppressed a shudder. 'Go and make that phone call then.'

He smiled. 'You're a game girl, Katie, I'll give you that.' The smile faded and for a moment, he looked very solemn. He glanced down at his watch and said in a low voice that she had to strain to hear 'I'm really very sorry.'

'Sorry? What for?'

For a moment, he looked blank, like old Mrs Simmons had that morning in the Salon when she'd lost track of the conversation in mid-sentence. 'Sorry — sorry for sacking you, of course,' he said, recovering himself quickly. 'It was all Gerald's fault, you know. He made me do it. I didn't want to. You were one of the best barmaids I've ever had. Would you like another drink while we're waiting?'

She shook her head. 'No. I'd better

keep a clear head,' she said with a smile.

'And is it? Clear, I mean. Is your head clear?' he asked.

'Sort of,' she said. 'Although I must admit, I feel like I've been put through a wringer. It's all the tension, I suppose.'

'Yes, that'll be it. Well, you sit there and relax while I call Gerald. I won't be a minute.'

★ ★ ★

Of course, she didn't relax. How could she? But she felt better knowing that Gerald could only get in through the back door and that he'd have to get past Donald first. But what if he attacked Donald? Gerald was twice his size and desperate. Poor Donald wouldn't stand a chance.

She took her phone from her pocket, ready to phone Will, as her nerve began to fail her again. Donald had said she was a game girl. A weird expression that made her sound a bit like a pheasant. But her gameness, if there was such a word, was just a front. She felt as wobbly as a kitten on a tightrope. And just about as weak. In fact, at the moment, she doubted if she could have stood up if she'd wanted to.

True to his word, Donald was soon back. Kat was slumped back in the chair, as the succession of disturbed nights coupled with the thought that she was probably doing the most dangerous — and foolish — thing she'd ever done in her life, left her feeling utterly drained.

'Is he coming?' she asked.

But instead of answering her question, Donald looked down at his watch again. 'It's taking longer than I thought,' he murmured. 'Although you're looking pretty sleepy now. I should have given you a larger dose.'

'What?' She sat up straight, her heart thumping, her head swimming. 'What are you talking about? What do you mean by a larger dose?'

'I mean a larger dose than I gave Doreen.' He picked up the baseball bat and tapped it into the palm of his hand in an edgy, staccato rhythm. 'Of course, you're that much younger than she was, so I suppose that would make a difference. I'm an idiot. I should have taken that into consideration.'

Kat couldn't take her eyes off the bat, that Donald was still tap-tapping into the palm of his hand. 'I — I don't understand,' she said weakly. 'What are you talking about?'

'The dose of sleeping draught I gave you was the same as the one I gave Doreen before I killed her. But never mind, it looks as if it's working now. There's no rush. I can wait.'

As he was speaking, he was caressing the baseball bat again, his usually bland, expressionless face transformed by a hideous smile.

20

Kat stared up at him in horror. Donald? Dippy Donald, the dull as ditchwater landlord who always faded into the background, was a murderer? Maybe even a double murderer? Surely not. It was far more likely that he was one of those sad people who confessed to crimes they hadn't committed in a bid to get attention. He couldn't even kill a spider and only last week had spent ages trying to persuade one that had been lurking in the bar to climb on to a piece of paper before carrying it safely outside.

'I don't believe you,' she said. 'You wouldn't — '

'Have the nerve? Is that what you think?' The manic edge to his yelp of laughter sent a shiver down Kat's spine. 'Which politician was it who said 'Never underestimate the determination of a quiet man'? Well, whoever it was, that's me. The quiet man who is very, very determined.'

'You're saying you killed Doreen? What about Marjorie? Was that down to you as well?' Kat asked and clapped her hand to her mouth as he nodded. 'But how?' she asked. 'Why?'

He still had the same scary smile on his face. 'I suppose I may as well tell you. It's not like you're going anywhere. So you might as well listen to a nice bedtime story while you're falling asleep. Are you sitting comfortably? Then I'll begin. Once upon a time, there was a nosy old witch, who went around the village making trouble for everyone she met. But one day, she went too far and made trouble for the wrong person. Because that person was very clever and he had a cunning plan.'

'You're mad,' Kat whispered.

'Damn right I was. Hopping mad. Time was critical, you see. I had just ten weeks, that's how long Joyce's cruise was, to put my plan in hand. And it would have worked, too, if it hadn't been for that nosy old bat. And if Gerald had held his nerve. It still can, in fact.'

'Gerald? Then he wasn't the murderer?'

Donald's laugh was no less manic the second time. 'He's a lily-livered fool who loses his nerve at the first sign of trouble.'

'Whereas you — ?'

'Whereas I am clever and resourceful and take my chances when they present themselves. Marjorie Hampton was about to ruin everything I'd worked for. Stupid, stupid woman. She'd found out Gerald was getting inside information from his contact in the Planning Department — '

'Doreen Spetchley,' Kat said before she could stop herself. So, Sean had been right about that. 'His contact was Doreen Spetchley, wasn't it? So they weren't having an affair?'

Donald grinned. 'Well, let's put it this way. She thought they were. The stupid woman actually believed him when he said that the money was for their new life together. Pathetic.' He thwacked the baseball bat into his palm with sickening relish. 'Anyway, she'd given Gerald the nod a few times. People in the planning office get to hear about upcoming deals long before they get as far as making a formal application for planning permission and

Gerald has had some nice little earners from that source over the years, I can tell you. And I'd just persuaded him to let me in on it, when Marjorie got wind of it and was threatening to ruin everything. So I'd got Gerald to arrange a meeting with her up at Millers Hill that afternoon.'

'So it was Gerald who Marjorie was going to meet after she'd seen John Manning. Gerald who'd got her dander up, as she'd put it?'

'Exactly. Only, of course, I was going to keep the appointment instead of him. He'd never have had the nerve to do what had to be done even though he was more than happy to take his cut of the proceeds. Whereas I not only had the nerve, but the resourcefulness too. I'd taken this,' Kat shrank away as he waved the baseball bat at her, 'And planned for her to have a little accident. But when I passed the Mannings' farm and heard her and John Manning going at it hammer and tongs, I couldn't believe my luck. I'd been wondering what to do with her body and suddenly, John Manning had handed me the solution on a plate — or, to be strictly accurate, a freezer.'

'Poor, poor Marjorie.' Kat gave a little whimper as the ever-present image of Marjorie, face down in that freezer, flashed into her mind. 'But how did you get her body to the Farm Shop? Surely someone would have seen you?'

'Stupid, interfering Majorie, more like,' he snorted. 'John Manning had run up a pretty big bar bill and, a couple of weeks earlier, had given me a spare key to the shop and told me to go in any time I was passing and help myself to anything I could find in the freezers up there in lieu of payment. I'd been carrying the key around for ages.'

'But how would that help you?' Kat really didn't want to know but she was playing for time. She didn't want to sit here, listening to him crowing about how he had got away with murder, but maybe if she could keep him talking —

'I met Marjorie up on Millers Hill as arranged and spun her a yarn about how she'd been quite right about the property scam Gerald had been involved in and that John Fleming was in on it with him.

She swallowed it hook, line and sinker. According to her, it explained why Fleming had been so aggressive to her. Anyway, I went on to say that I'd confronted Fleming who'd agreed to meet us at the Farm Shop where he'd give us evidence that would put Gerald Crabshaw away for a long time. I was able to show her the key that Fleming had given me and of course, she'd agreed like a shot.'

'Poor, poor Marjorie,' Kat murmured again. Her brain had frozen. It was the only thing she could think to say.

'Poor Marjorie, my eye,' he snorted. 'Interfering old baggage, more like it. I'd put every penny I had to buy that land and when it goes through, I'll be away from this miserable place and my miserable wife faster than you can say knife. Have you any idea what it's like to be married to someone like her? She's the one with the money, you know, and there isn't a day goes by where she doesn't remind me of that fact.'

'But you could have just left her. There's no need to — ' Kat looked at him, her eyes full of horror. 'Oh God, you haven't killed her as well, have you?'

He shook his head. 'Not yet. But it may well come to that. Now I'm getting the hang of it, as it were. Drugs are wonderful, don't you agree? I gave Doreen the same as I gave you. She just went to sleep and didn't know a thing about it. It was all very humane.'

Kat shifted uncomfortably in her chair. There was no doubt he was as mad as a box of frogs but he was clever with it. He'd played the part of an unremarkable, grey man to perfection. While all the time, inside, he was a cold calculating monster who'd stop at nothing to achieve his aims.

'She walked into that shop like a lamb to the slaughter,' he chortled. 'Get it? Lamb to the slaughter? And you'll never guess what I hit her with?'

'The baseball bat?' Kat said, unable to take her eyes off it.

'Wrong. It made me laugh when I heard about the amount of time the police spent looking for the murder weapon. Do you remember that brilliant Roald Dahl story where this woman hit her husband over the head with a frozen leg of lamb, which she then cooked and served up to the policemen who came to investigate?'

Kat felt sick as she remembered the night after Marjorie's body had been found. There'd been roast lamb on the specials board.

'It would have been perfect,' Donald went on. 'I'd planned to tip her into one of the freezers and chances are, it would have been months, maybe even years before she was found. But, unfortunately, someone came along and tried the door, just at the wrong time.'

'That would have been John,' Kat said but he wasn't listening.

'I had to leave her there, half in, half out and leg it.' He laughed again, like he was having the time of his life. 'Do you get it, Katie? I said leg it. And I did just that. Legged it with the leg of lamb I'd bashed her over the head with and cooked it, here in the pub. Just like in that story. Went down a treat as the next day's Special, if you remember. The pub was heaving.'

Kat didn't want to think of roast lamb any more. In fact, she didn't think she'd ever be able to eat it again. Time, she reckoned, for a change of subject.

'But why did you kill Doreen? What did she ever do to you?'

'That was Gerald's fault. I told you he was a lily-livered fool, didn't I? He'd been keeping her sweet for years and, over that time, she'd come up with some pretty good stuff for him, including that supermarket development in Dintscombe. He made a right killing there. I overheard him boasting about it one night and told him that I wanted in on the next one, or else. Well, he caved in, of course and this one, up on Miller's Hill, that's going to be huge and earn us both enough shedloads of money. Enough to take me a long, long way away from here.'

'Develop Miller's Hill? There's no way the council will ever agree to that.'

He smiled. 'Want to bet? Trouble was, Doreen was getting cold feet and told Gerald she wanted out. Gerald lost his head and tried to break things off with her, stupid idiot. Because that just made her more determined than ever to blow the whistle.' He broke off and looked at Kat closely. 'How come you're still awake? Maybe you should have another glass of malt. One for the road, as it were.'

'N-not really awake,' Kat slurred, her words stumbling over each other. 'V-very s-sleepy.'

'Thank God for that. Because I'm afraid, my dear, story time is almost over. The wicked witch is dead. So too the ugly old stepsister. And, any day now, I shall be living happily ever after. While you, I'm afraid — '

'Wh-what are you going to do with me?' Kat managed to ask. 'Not . . . farm shop freezers. Still — still c-crawling with police.'

'Didn't I say I had it all planned? This pub has a very old cellar with a nice old-fashioned dirt floor.'

'D-don't like s-spiders,' Kat managed to say, her leaden eyelids closing, as she slid down in the chair.

21

'That's it.' He lunged forward, grabbed her arm and peered closely at her. 'You're looking nice and sleepy now. Don't fight it, Katie. It'll be easier — '

He didn't get any further. It's difficult to talk when you're suddenly face-down on the floor, with one arm twisted behind you and a knee in the small of your back.

'Did I forget to put on my CV that I learnt judo at college?' she asked, a little breathlessly. 'I was actually quite good at it.'

Another thing she forgot to mention was that her Media Studies course had included a Drama module and one of the things they'd been taught was how to make it look like you're drinking when you're not. Useful when you're on stage and don't want to splutter cold tea over your fellow actors.

Kat had used the trick to pretend she was drinking the whisky Donald poured for her (she doubted whether the poor spider plant on the shelf behind her would ever recover from being drowned in the finest malt whisky) because that first sip had tasted so awful but she hadn't wanted to hurt Donald's feelings by saying so.

Weird to think it may well have saved her life. He must have put enough in to knock out a horse as the tiny amount she'd had had begun to affect her, although she had, of course, exaggerated her symptoms when she realised what he was up to, in the hope that it would put him off guard.

And it had worked beautifully. Except for one small thing. What the hell did she do now? OK, Donald couldn't move. But neither could she.

Her phone was in her pocket but to reach it she'd have to release her hold on his arm. The front door was locked and the back door looked miles away. If she made a dash for it, he'd get her before she reached it. And — this was the bit that made her blood run cold — he was a whole lot closer to that lethal baseball bat than she was and she knew for certain he wouldn't hesitate to use it.

What she needed now, she thought desperately, as he wriggled, squirmed and cursed beneath her, was a minor miracle. Correction: a major miracle. John Wayne swooping over the horizon with the cavalry would be good.

Then, as if someone up there had been listening, came a loud banging on the front door.

'Help me!' she yelled. 'Come round the back! Quickly.'

After what seemed a lifetime, the door was flung open. It wasn't John Wayne who stood there but Gerald Crabshaw. She groaned and slackened her hold on Donald's arm as she realised it was all over for her.

She didn't resist as he pulled her away. All the fight had left her and she slumped to the floor.

'I'm so sorry, Katie,' he said. 'I tried to warn you — '

'Keep her there, Crabshaw,' Donald panted as he struggled to get up. 'While I fetch — '

His words ended in a scream as Will's

foot came down hard on Donald's outstretched arm. Thank God. Not the cavalry after all but something much better. Will. Where had he come from? Kat could only think he'd come in behind Gerald. And thank goodness he had. Talk about perfect timing. If she'd been the sort to swoon, she would surely have swooned then. Instead, she pushed Gerald away and snatched up the baseball bat.

'OK, you. Get over there and don't move,' she said. 'I'm calling the police.'

'There's no need,' Gerald said. 'They're on their way. I'd already called them when I saw Will. Please, Katie, put that thing down. I'm on your side. Ask Will.'

'Well, I would,' she said, never letting the bat drop for one second. 'But he's a bit busy with your partner in crime at the moment. So stay back.'

'Will. Tell her please,' Gerald said. 'Tell her how I drove up to your farm and asked you to come down to the pub with me because she was in danger.'

Will had, by this time, got Donald face-down on the floor again. But this time

Donald must have known he was well beaten for he made no attempt to struggle free, probably because to do so would probably result in a dislocated shoulder, owing to the pressure Will was applying to his arm.

'He's telling the truth,' Will said. 'I must admit, I thought he'd flipped or something. Couldn't make head nor tail of what he was saying. But when he said you were in danger, I thought I'd better come along and check it out. Just in case.'

'Thank goodness you did.' Kat had, by this time, started to shake as the reaction set in. 'He — he was going to kill me, you know.'

Donald screamed as Will gave his arm an extra hard tug.

'Please, Will. Don't,' she begged. 'There's been more than enough violence around here and I really don't think I can stand any more. If, as you say, the police are on the way — '

'I called them,' Gerald said. 'I want you to know that. I never meant things to get this far, and when you told me just now that Doreen's death hadn't been an accident, I knew I had to put a stop to it.'

Kat rounded on him, the baseball bat still raised. 'You didn't try very hard,' she said. 'Just shouted something after me then drove off. And you were part of the plan to get me here in the first place, weren't you? All that talk about giving me a story of the century? That was just a ploy to get me here so that Donald here could — '

'I thought he was just going to frighten you into leaving things alone,' Gerald said. 'That's what he said. But after you told me about Doreen I tried to stop you coming in here, Katie. Just you remember that. So I drove off to get help,' he glanced at his watch. 'I told the police it was urgent. I — I had nothing to do with those women's deaths, you know. I didn't know what he'd done. He just said he was going to sort Marjorie out. I — I thought he meant he had some dirt on her and was going to blackmail her into backing off. That's how he got to me, you know. Blackmail.'

'Shut up, you fool,' Donald snarled.

'You've called me a fool for the last

time,' Gerald said. 'When the police get here I'm going to tell them everything. At first, I really believed John Manning had killed Marjorie — I'm sorry about that, Will — but when Katie told me they'd let him go, I started thinking about how Donald had gone up to Millers Hill that afternoon to meet her although he said she never turned up. So I came to the pub to challenge him.'

'That would be when Elsie Flintlock overheard you,' Kat said. 'Donald told her that you'd been running up a bar bill. And that was what you'd had words about.'

'Which is nothing but the truth,' Donald said, although his voice was a bit muffled. 'Look, Will, let me up, will you, so that I can explain? It's not fair that this crook should be allowed to push the blame on to me. And after all, I'm not going anywhere, am I?'

'Too right you're not,' Will said, as he let Donald move into a sitting position.

'Thanks.' He glared up at Gerald. 'Let's face it, Crabshaw, you're the one who's been breaking the law here, with your dodgy little land deals. What was it? Did

Doreen Spetchley threaten to blow the whistle on you? The way that Marjorie Hampton did?'

'How dare you try and pin it on me?' Gerald protested, his face scarlet. 'I'll own up to the property scams, yes. But as for the rest of it — '

'As for the rest of it, it's my word against yours,' Donald said smoothly.

'Hardly,' Kat said. 'There's the small matter of you trying to drug me. I'm sure the police will find traces of whatever it was you slipped into my drink in that poor plant over there, which is where, luckily for me, most of it ended up. And then, of course, there's this. I recorded every word you said.'

She reached into her pocket and took out her phone.

'I always said you were a bright girl, Katie Latcham,' Gerald said but she ignored him and focussed on Donald who was staring at her with cold, hate filled eyes.

'It's all here,' she said, forcing herself not to flinch under that malevolent stare. 'About how you killed Marjorie. And, of course, your little bedtime story about the frozen leg of lamb. Remember? Not to mention what you did to poor Doreen. Do you want to listen to it while we wait for the police?'

As it turned out, there wasn't time, as she was interrupted by the sound of approaching sirens. The cavalry had arrived at last.

Will, still holding Donald, turned to her and smiled. Big, solid dependable Will, with his rugby player shoulders and gloriously sexy blue eyes. Why had she never noticed them in that way before? And what on earth was she doing thinking about it now, of all times?

★ ★ ★

Kat and Will stood, side by side, and watched as the police cars drove away, Donald, stony-faced and silent in one and Gerald, talking his head off in the other.

'The policeman was quite right, you know,' he said.

'Which policeman?'

'The one who said you were all sorts of

an idiot for getting yourself in this situation in the first place.' He glared at her and shook his head. 'Honestly, Katie, I could — '

'It's Kat. And he didn't call me an idiot. In fact, if you remember, he said it was very resourceful of me to record Donald the way I did.'

'But he meant idiot.' He took her hand and turned to face her, his eyes serious. 'When I think what could have happened. If I hadn't been in the yard when Gerald arrived. If we'd been a few minutes later getting here. If . . . '

Gently, she took her hand from his and placed it on his lips to stop him. She didn't want to think about what might have happened. Didn't want to go any further down that particular road. Not now. Not ever.

'But you were there,' she said, her voice husky. 'You were there for me, just like you've always been.'

'Just like I always will be.'

Kat's breath caught in her throat, her fingers where they rested on his mouth, felt as if they were melting. What was going on here? This was Will, remember? Her almost brother. The guy who used to call her Scaredy Cat, who'd tied her plaits to the back of her chair. The guy with the sexy blue eyes and the most kissable mouth she'd ever seen.

Why had she not noticed that before? If she took her hand away and lifted her head just a fraction . . .

It was the sweetest, the gentlest, the most un-brotherly kiss that turned her knees to water and left her clinging to him, scarcely able to breathe. She murmured a protest as he pulled away, his eyes questioning. Was she sure? She'd never been more sure about anything in her life. All that rubbish about how weird it would be to kiss the man she'd grown up thinking of as her brother was just that. Rubbish.

Certainly there was nothing remotely sisterly about the way she answered his unspoken question by wrapping both arms around the back of his neck and kissing him back. Only this time, the kiss was deeper, more urgent and wiped everything else from her mind.

She forgot about Donald and his

murderous ways, about Gerald and his dodgy land deals. Even about her mum and what she would say when she found out. With Will's arms around her, she felt safe and comforted. Like she had come home. And it felt so, so good.

Until she remembered what Jules had told her.

'The vet,' she said, as she pulled away.

'What?' He looked dazed, like she'd just woken him up.

'Your sexy Swedish vet. Jules told me that you and she — '

He laughed. 'Anneka is in her mid-forties and happily married to Sven. I think Jules may have been winding you up. Why do you ask? Were you jealous?'

'What me? No, of course not. It was just that I — ' she broke off, looked up at that very kissable mouth again and decided it was time for the truth — even though it had taken her for ever to realise it was the truth. 'Of course I was jealous, you oaf.'

'Good,' he said as he bent to kiss her again. 'Now you know how I felt when I saw you with that smooth Irishman. And as for — '

'Well, and here was me thinking I'd missed all the excitement.' Elsie Flintlock's voice made them both whirl round. 'About time, too. I must say, Will Manning, you took your time. I was beginning to despair of you.'

'Oh God,' Kat moaned as she watched Elsie walk off, cackling away to herself. 'That'll be all round the village in a nanosecond.'

'Do you mind?' Will asked, his arms still around her.

Kat shook her head. Why would she? Everything was more than all right with her world now. Donald and Gerald were 'helping the police with their enquiries'. She had a brilliant story to take to the editor tomorrow. And she'd lost an 'almost' brother and gained gorgeous, sexy Will who was without doubt the best kisser on the planet.

The only tiny cloud on her horizon was how to convince her mother that she never, ever wanted to eat roast lamb ever again.

THE END

We do hope that you have enjoyed reading this large print book.

Did you know that all of our titles are available for purchase?

We publish a wide range of high quality large print books including:
Romances, Mysteries, Classics
General Fiction
Non Fiction and Westerns

Special interest titles available in large print are:
The Little Oxford Dictionary
Music Book, Song Book
Hymn Book, Service Book

Also available from us courtesy of Oxford University Press:
Young Readers' Dictionary
(large print edition)
Young Readers' Thesaurus
(large print edition)

For further information or a free brochure, please contact us at:
Ulverscroft Large Print Books Ltd.,
The Green, Bradgate Road, Anstey,
Leicester, LE7 7FU, England.
Tel: (00 44) **0116 236 4325**
Fax: (00 44) **0116 234 0205**

THE BLACK CHARADE

John Burke

Dr. Caspian and his wife Bronwen, both possessed of genuine psychic powers, have gained a reputation as investigators of so-called psychic phenomena, exposing a number of fraudulent mediums. They are consulted by prominent politician Joseph Hinde, whose daughter Laura has become strangely withdrawn. He suspects she may be attending séances in an attempt to contact her dead mother. Asked to rescue her from the clutches of evil charlatans, the Caspians' investigations uncover a trail of people dying in strange and horrible circumstances . . .